WHEN JESUS HEALS

A Christian Novel

Linda Swann

CHAPTER 1

The Jones Family

Greg woke to a warm June morning wrapped in sunshine. It was 6:00, his usual time to get up. He hadn't used an alarm clock in years. It was his internal clock that woke him and his enthusiasm that impelled him out of bed. He was inspired by the thought of a new day, a blank canvas, a fresh sheet of paper that he could fill with anything he wanted. Today was an important day at the office. He and his friend Roger would present an idea to the CEO that could change their lives and the lives of their families.

He looked at his wife, sleeping peacefully beside him. She was so beautiful lying there with her shiny blond hair contrasting the burgundy pillowcase and the blankets pulled up to her chin. Greg felt the desire to wake her but decided against it. He knew she would need her rest for the long day ahead.

Greg slipped quietly out of bed and walked softly into the bathroom. He always looked good, even when he just got out of bed. He looked at himself in the mirror. He was six foot three with light brown hair and striking amber eyes. His face was naturally handsome with a firm jaw and laugh lines. He had a trim, muscular figure, the kind of man that women like. He finished in the bathroom and started down the hall.

The bedroom doors were closed, the kids sleeping quietly. The first room he passed was Janet's. He was so proud of her.

Janet was everything he ever wanted in a daughter. She was so cute, so smart and accomplished. She had the determination to do anything she wanted, and she could do nothing wrong as far as he was concerned. She had always been a happy child, fascinated by everything. Now at age fourteen she was growing into a young lady. Greg was in awe of her transformation as he had been since the day she was born.

The next room he came to was Jason's. He was tall and handsome, just like his father. Jason had gone to a teen dance the night before, coming in past curfew. It was unusual for him to be late. Greg was sure to hear an interesting excuse later. "I'll go easy on him," Greg thought. He's seventeen and almost a man. It's time for him to start making some of his own decisions."

The youngest, Cindy, was eight now. Greg and Faith had only wanted two children. When Cindy came along Faith had to put her career on hold again. But Cindy turned out to be a beautiful child. She was all smiles and curls, a true blessing.

Greg continued down the stairs through the living room and into the kitchen. He opened the cabinet and took out the coffee beans. The smell of fresh ground coffee permeated the kitchen. Greg started the coffee maker and then looked around. Faith took pride in their house, and it was beautiful and immaculate. She had remodeled this room when Cindy was a baby and chose custom made teak cabinets and granite counter tops. Greg felt a sense of peace and fulfillment when he looked at all he and Faith had accomplished. His life was perfect, and it was about to get even better, he thought.

Life was good to him. Nature had given him good looks and his parents had given him an Ivy League education and high social standing. Greg had taken those advantages and made a wonderful life for himself. He worked hard for what he had, and he deserved it. He knew that he was envied by his peers. He tried to be a good person and his family went to church on Sunday. He gave his

10% to the Church as he should and even gave more at Christmas. He had the picture-perfect life that they strived for, and he liked knowing that he was better than most.

Greg decided to take advantage of the quiet house to go over his presentation. He gathered his laptop and papers and took them out the French doors to sit on the patio by the pool. He was confident in his speaking ability and the idea he and his partner, Roger, had been working on for months. Greg believed there was a need for a new marketing department at his firm. Right now, the work was distributed between several people in different departments and the advertising agency they worked with. The idea was to create a new branch to take responsibility for the whole process. He and Roger believed it could be done with minimal costs and save the company overtime expenses and increase income. If everything went well, he could look forward to a promotion and a raise. His company was fair and rewarded employees who increased profits.

This next promotion would allow him and his family to live comfortably for the rest of their lives. His children would go to the best colleges. Maybe they could even move to one of the new houses by the golf course. Their present neighbors were nice people but most of them were, well, common, for lack of a better word.

The couple that lived to their right were religious fanatic. They sent their children to the Christian Academy. They did not trim their house out at Christmas like everyone else. They only had a nativity scene in the yard. Their daughter, Carol was not allowed to wear the latest styles and make up. True, those styles were a little skimpy, but kids always dress different than their parents would like them to when they are becoming independent. He did not intend to stand in the way of his kids maturing into adults. His philosophy was that you must let your kids make their own choices, so they can learn.

The people on their left did not keep their lawn up to his standards. Their hedges were not trimmed, and the flower beds often had weeds growing in them. Why couldn't they just hire a landscaper? But Bill ran an auto repair shop and his wife worked in the office at the school. They probably couldn't afford yard help.

His thoughts were interrupted when Faith came from the kitchen.

"Good morning," Faith said as she drew up a chair and put her coffee cup down. "Why didn't you wake me? I have to be at the club early."

"You looked so peaceful, I just couldn't wake you up," Greg said.

Faith was the director at the Country Club Health Spa. Being a wife and a mother had kept her from pursuing her dream of traveling abroad to design and establish overseas health clubs for Metropolitan Spas. But she liked her job, and it was challenging in a way. A couple of years after Cindy was born, she had started to feel trapped in a mundane existence as a stay-at-home parent. That was when she found Helen, the most wonderful nanny and housekeeper. With Helen taking over most of the housekeeping and chauffeur duties, Faith was free to pursue her own career. She knew her children gained more than they lost from her absence because she was a happier person when she had outside interests and Helen added so much to their lives.

"Well, I'd better do my laps. I'll be interviewing new instructors today. A bunch of young girls who probably don't have the slightest idea of the stamina required to teach aerobics. Have you heard anything from the kids?"

"No, do you think we should wake them?" Greg asked.

"It's summer, let them sleep. Helen can wake then when she comes," replied Faith.

"Don't forget we're going over to Roger and Alice's tonight for dinner to celebrate. We're sure to have a successful meeting today and we want to brag to our wives a little," said Greg.

"I'm glad you reminded me; we're getting ready for the stockholders meeting at the club. I'll be working late but I should be able to get home by 8:00. What time are we expected for dinner?

Roger said Alice planned dinner for 9:00. We all have a full day today, but we wanted to get together anyway."

9:00 is a little tight but we should be able to pull it off," she said. It was the first time he was getting home early in months, and she was looking forward to an evening out with friends.

Greg and Faith were always busy and happy. Sometimes it seemed like something was missing but there wasn't any time to think about it, much less fit anything else into their already busy schedules.

"Well, I need to get ready," said Greg.

"Okay, honey, I'll see you upstairs after my laps."

Faith cared deeply about looking thin and healthy. She was faithful to her diet and exercise regimen. She knew it was her looks that had opened many doors for her. It was her beauty that attracted Greg to her 20 years ago and it was her self-discipline that allowed her to control her busy lifestyle. Without beauty, fitness and discipline she knew she would have nothing.

She finished her laps and went upstairs. Greg was putting on his tie and Faith noticed it was crooked. She squeezed in between him and the mirror to straighten it. She knew how important today was to him and wanted him to look perfect. She loved looking at him.

Greg and Faith said their goodbyes in the bedroom. They wouldn't be making those "just to say hi" calls or meeting for lunch like they used to. That kind of intimacy had stopped some time ago when Greg and Roger started working on this project. But Greg often sent flowers and Faith knew how lucky she was.

Faith showered and stood in the walk-in closet deciding what to wear. She chose a simple neutral pants suit. She would be doing interviews for new instructors today and would need to be dressed professionally. Her blond hair cascaded over her shoulders. Her eyes were a perfect gleaming green and stood out from the suit. She wore minimal makeup, just enough to enhance her natural beauty. One last look to make sure she looked perfect, and she was ready for the day. Faith checked on each of her children on the way down the hall. They were all sleeping peacefully. She knew Helen would be there in half an hour.

Faith went out to the three-car garage. Greg's sports car was gone. The SUV for the family which Helen usually drove was parked beside her new champagne colored hybrid coupe. As she headed down the driveway, she felt like she was at a crossroads, and nothing would be the same after today. Life was good and about to get a better, she thought.

Helen arrived, as always, at 8:00. She had been working at the Jones' for more than 7 years. She lived on the other side of town and Faith had tried to talk her into moving into the maids' quarters, behind the kitchen. But Helen was a born again Christian and very much involved in her community and church. While she felt comfortable working with this family, she did not share their lifestyle and would never say it, but she needed the companionship of other Christians that felt the same way as she did about living a life dedicated to the ideals that Christ himself dictated.

Helen had made many mistakes with her own kids. Her commitment to God came after they were grown and gone. She used to be a lot like the Jones Family, believing but not committed. Now Helen welcomed the chance to make a difference in someone else's' life. She knew in her heart that the Lord meant for her to be here, working for the Jones family. She had never witnessed to them. She just let them know her viewpoint then worked to live up to it. She wasn't perfect to be sure.

She knew that Greg had been able to trust her easier because of her religious point of view while at the same time thinking less of her for being a "fanatic". Helen always felt that the Jones' were wonderful people groping in the dark. Nothing she did could alter that. But she felt that she contributed to this family in a positive way, and she was both humbled and blessed to be part of their life.

The Jones were neat, orderly people. Greg and Faith insisted that the kids pick up after themselves, so Helen never walked into a messy home. She did the cooking, cleaning, laundry, took care of the kids and drove them to activities. And often took the place of Greg and Faith on the bleachers or in the auditorium at events.

But she didn't mind. She loved these kids and was proud of their achievements.

Cindy was the first to get up around 8:30. "Morning Helen, where are Mommy and Daddy?"

"They left early this morning; I'm making blueberry muffins. Are you hungry?"

"I guess so. I wanted to tell Mommy about my gymnastics award and see if I can go to the Statesville competition. Do think they'll come? Maybe I can call her. I have to get the permission slip signed. Do you know when they're coming home?"

"Slow down, little one", said Helen. I'm sure we can figure something out. Your mom told me that she and your dad both have meetings this morning and I don't think they'll be able to answer the phone. We can try to call after lunch, and I'm sure you'll see them both after work tonight."

"I've been waiting since yesterday. I want to call. They'll stop their meeting and talk to me!"

"You may be right, Cindy. But these meetings are important for the whole family. You need to have a little more patience. Let's find something to keep your mind occupied for now. You can help me pick out something nice for dinner. And we can work on knots for your Girl Scout badge, too. Before you know it will be lunchtime and you can call your mom."

"Okay", Cindy frowned. She was a good girl and had learned to live with disappointment.

Janet was the next to appear around 11:00. She was showered and perfumed and wearing her new bikini. Her makeup was tasteful if a little heavy in Helen's opinion. Janet had learned to apply it well and always looked fresh and flawless. But Helen thought she had no business wearing a suit like that, especially at her age. She was 14 years old but looked like she was 18, or older.

"Good morning, sunshine. We're having blueberry muffins and fruit for breakfast. Are you hungry?"

"Not yet, Helen, I'm expecting the gang, soon. They are going to stay for lunch and hang out this afternoon. Is that okay with you? Mom said she didn't think you'd mind. We arranged it last night after you'd gone.

"Of course, I don't mind. But you could at least have a glass of juice."

I want to get in the pool. I'll have something at lunch, I promise."

Helen watched Janet step gingerly into the pool. Eating was a daily struggle between them. Janet didn't appear to eat enough to keep a bird alive. She skipped meals every day and when she did eat it was only a few bites. Helen had talked to Faith about it, but Faith was so happy that she had such a beautiful family and that she didn't have to worry about the children's weight. All Helen could do was to provide the family with good, healthy food and encourage Janet to eat it. The rest was in God's hands, and it had become customary many years ago for Helen to thank God for this family and learn to leave them in His hands. It was another lesson from this job, and another blessing

Jason came down after noon looking tousled. He had been to the Country Club under twenty-one dance with friends the night before. After the dance they went to Jeremy's house, whose parents were away for the weekend. They had paired off, each couple taking a bedroom. Jason and his girl fell asleep in each other's arms for a couple of hours, and he didn't get home until after 1:00. He would have to come up with something to tell his dad. He would stay as close to the truth as possible and leave out the details that his dad would object to.

Jason was 6'2" and the kind of boy that any parent would be proud of. He was one of the most handsome young men in the town with dark blond hair and unusual light brown eyes like his father. He was muscular with an easy stance, straight back and broad shoulders. He was respectful, personable and nice, the kind of boy that people wanted to be around. And Jason liked being the center of attention. He was on the football team at school and was looking forward to his senior year. This year he would be one of the players the college scouts were looking at. The girls would all want to be with him. It had always been that way but as a senior he would be at the top of the food chain. He had found few partners when he was 14 and 15, but at 17 he wasn't lacking in willing girls. Most of his peers were sexually active and he had a reputation for being skilled and gentle.

"Good morning, Helen", he yawned. He probably shouldn't have had that beer last night, he thought. He often "just said no." But every once in a while he indulged, just to fit in with the others. It wasn't that his friends teased him about not drinking, not anymore, he just didn't want them to think he was judging them. He found the loss of control caused by alcohol to be uncomfortable. That was probably why he fell asleep and why he was groggy now.

"What's for breakfast?" He knew he was too late for breakfast, but he gave Helen a chance to tell him that.

"We had blueberry muffins and fruit hours ago. Lunch is almost ready and I'm serving it by the pool." Helen retorted, smiling.

"If I knew you were making your blueberry muffins, I'd have gotten up sooner. Can I have one for an appetizer?"

"Of course, Jason, they're on the counter, help yourself."

Jason grabbed a muffin and sauntered out to the patio. He loved looking at Janet's young friends. And he knew he was one of the reasons they looked perfect in their bikinis and make up.

Their neighbor Carol was getting ready to dive. Carol was pretty in a way, but she wasn't one of those girls who tried to look perfect. She wore her YWCA swim team suit which was not sexy and never wore makeup like the other girls that came over. There was something about Carol that suggested inner depth and self-respect along with the attitude that she didn't care what others thought that appealed to Jason, in a way. She wasn't provocative or flirty; she was more like one of the guys. And with Carol being an athlete, too, they had started an easy-going friendship, his first with a girl.

He would talk to Carol and watch superfluously while the other girls giggled and tried to get his attention. Then just as they were becoming discouraged, he would turn on his charm and watch as they succumbed.

The afternoon was warm and happy, like many other summer days. They were proud of their home and pool. They were proud that their housekeeper made great snacks and treated their friends like they were welcomed. Other housekeepers were obviously put out when friends visited. But Helen always seemed happy to have the kids there. Janet and Jason knew it was one of the reasons everyone wanted to come to their house.

While the teens played and swam, Helen helped Cindy work on learning knots for her Girl Scout badge. Cindy was distracted and frustrated.

"Here, honey, just do what it says one step at a time. This end goes over then under and then through…"

"I can't do it"

"You can do it. Just take your time and follow the directions."

"I don't want to! I want to go swimming."

Helen thought swimming might be just the thing to vent some of Cindy's frustrations.

"Okay, honey, go get your suit on. We'll work on this later."

Helen wondered about Cindy's attitude and put it down to her frustration over not being able to call her parents. Poor kid, she worked so hard for that second place. She's only eight. I can't blame her for being impatient.

She glanced out from time to time and watched as the young women played with Cindy. "They are such good kids," she thought.

These were days of innocence and ease, but the teens didn't know it. The day was blissful for all of them. The kids had a great time. The sounds of laughter and play were like beautiful music to Helen. It invoked joy in her heart. She sang as she worked and soon it was time for dinner.

Faith called while they were eating and told her to go ahead and leave at 7:00. It was strange how little Helen saw the parents of these children she was helping to raise. But they were the employers and the arrangement seemed to work fine for them.

Helen cleaned up the kitchen and started the dishwasher.

She was tired in a pleasant way. The kind of tired you get when you put in a full day doing something you like. She checked on the kids before she left. Janet was in the den watching TV, Jason was out on the patio and Cindy was in her room.

"What are you doing?" asked Helen as she walked into Cindy's room.

"I'm playing games." Cindy had gotten a TV for her room on her birthday. It came complete with a game system which kept Cindy occupied when everyone else was busy.

Helen got Cindy her pajamas and reminded her to brush her teeth. "Okay, big hug," she said. The young girl seemed to need affection and Helen was happy to give it. She had come to love Cindy dearly over the years. She kissed Cindy's cheek and said goodnight.

Helen had missed her own children terribly when they were gone and ministering to Cindy helped ease the empty space in her heart. She had a great relationship to her own kids. They went to the same church and got together often. Her grandkids were a true blessing. But Cindy's obvious need for love opened a door in Helen's heart and filled a need of hers to give love. She always enjoyed children and her life seemed incomplete without them.

Helen left after 7:30. She often stayed later than Faith told her to. She didn't mind. She was responsible for these kids and would not leave until she knew they were okay and that their parents would be there very soon.

"Good night Jason, goodnight Janet. See ya tomorrow," Helen called on her way out the door.

CHAPTER 2

Greg and Faith

"Honey, I'm home," called Greg. It was 7:45, he had passed Helen just pulling out the driveway.

"Hi, dad," said Janet. She was in the den watching TV.

"Hi, honey. Where's mom?"

"She called to say she was on her way and that Helen should go home. She left Jason in charge. Can you let him know you're here so he'll stop bossing us around? And Cindy has something real important to talk to you and mom about.

She's been bugging us about it all day. She's up in her room getting ready for bed or something."

Sure. Did you kids eat supper?" He really wished Helen would just give up her apartment and move into the maid's rooms next to the kitchen. But he long ago accepted that she needed her own space and he respected that.

"Yeah, all done and cleaned up. Helen said you and mom are going out for dinner."

"We're going to Roger and Alice's to celebrate closing a very important deal today."

"That's great, dad. Congratulations."

"Thanks." He looked at his beautiful daughter and saw a

caring and intelligent young lady. Greg knew he and Faith had done something right. But he didn't remember being so grown up at their age. Times change, he thought.

"I'm going to get my shower. We'll have to hurry if we don't want to be late."

"Okay, dad." What's new, she thought.

Faith arrived a few minutes later. "Hi, Janet, how was your day?"

Great, mom. The gang came over and we just hung out around the pool. Dad's home. He's in the shower."

"Jason's out by the pool talking on his cell. He's been a pain ever since Helen left. He thinks I should do anything he wants just because all the other girls do. And Cindy's been bugging us all day about something she needs to tell you and dad. Helen wouldn't let her call because you had meetings today or something. She's up in her room getting ready for bed, I think."

"Okay, thanks," said Faith.

She went out to the patio, waved hello to Jason and headed up the stairs. She would have to hurry or they would be late. She stuck her head in the bathroom to say hi to Greg and started picking out her clothes. She chose a black dress, jade and silver earrings and necklace, black nylons and heels. It was an informal dinner with friends, thank goodness, because she wasn't going to have much time to do her hair.

"MOM!" Cindy flew into the room. "I got second place at the gymnastics meet yesterday! I had to wait all day to tell you!"

"Oh, honey, that's ok. You'll do better next time," said Faith distractedly.

"But, mom, Mr. Laugherty said I did great. I get to go to the Statesville competition! Can I! Will you and daddy come?"

"When is it?" asked Faith.

"It's in September. Can I go?"

"Maybe, Honey. We'll have to look at the calendar and I just don't have time right now."

"But, mom, I waited all day. I was practicing patience," cried Cindy.

"Honey, we have two months before September. Things are just a little crazy right now and you'll have to give me a few days to look at the calendar and read over the papers. Now, daddy and I are late for dinner at Roger and Alice's. I promise, we'll talk about this tomorrow. Right now we have to get ready and go."

"Can't you just tell me if I can go?"

"Probably, honey, but we'll have to wait and see for sure. I'm sorry you didn't win. I know you worked hard for the meet. You're lucky to have such a good coach. Would you like to help me get ready?"

"You look nice," Cindy said sadly. "I'm going to my room and read."

"I'll tuck you in before we leave," said Faith.

"Okay," Cindy walked back to her room.

Minutes later Faith didn't see any light coming from the space under Cindy's door. She opened it quietly and called softly but got no response. "She must be sleeping," Faith thought. But Cindy was laying in the dark crying, utterly dejected, angry and confused.

Minutes later Greg and Faith breezed out the door calling goodbye and good night to Janet and Jason. "In bed by 11:00, kids."

"All right," they called in unison from different rooms.

Janet had been expecting a confrontation between her parents and Jason. And while she didn't really want her brother to get into trouble, there was a small part of her that was vindicated by the thought that perfect Jason had done something wrong.

After her parents left she went out by the pool. "I can't believe they didn't even ask you about last night. If it was me, they'd have been in the living room waiting for me to get home."

"I'm older and I'm a boy," said Jason. He knew he'd have to explain what happened but the longer they waited to ask, the shorter the explanation could be.

"What's that got to do with it" Janet asked. "Rules are rules."

"Yeah, but I can't get pregnant," he said.

"You're such a jerk. I wonder what they'd do if they knew you're sleeping around. Maybe you can't get pregnant, but you can get other things."

"You'd better never say anything about what I do. And I won't tell them what you and your friends talk about." Jason knew neither of them would rat on the other. They loved each other. He had figured out last year that he and his sister had a unique relationship, and he could count on her.

"You know I got your back, Jason," Janet said.

"Yeah, I know."

On the way to dinner, Greg and Faith were having a rare moment to talk uninterrupted.

"I'm glad to put this project behind us. Maybe we can spend more time together. I miss you, Greg. I know the kids do, too."

"And I miss you," he said.

"I'm concerned about Jason," said Faith. "He was out until after twelve last night."

"I don't think we need to worry about Jason."

"We'll need to confront him about it. We can't just let him start making his own curfew. If we let him do it, we'll have to do the same for the girls. I think he needs some consequences for breaking the rules."

"I agree, he does need consequences, but I don't think we need to worry about it. He's growing up and it's good for him to make some of his own choices, and his own mistakes."

"I'm sure you're right. It makes me very uncomfortable to think of him experimenting with drugs and alcohol or sex. I knew that he would be faced with these things as a teenager, but wasn't it just last week that he was eight years old and all he wanted in the world was our approval?"

"Greg chuckled. "I guess those days are over. It makes me wonder about Cindy, though. She doesn't seem to be making the same effort as the other kids did."

"She's okay," said Faith. She lost a gymnastics meet. She came in second and I know she must be disappointed. She's different than Jason and Janet. She's more introverted and self-reliant. They're all good kids. I think we're lucky to have such beautiful, well-adjusted children, especially these days."

"I know you're right. I'm so glad that I'm going to be able to send them to good colleges. They won't have to struggle with living expenses and tuition like we did.

"I'm glad your project went well, and I'm glad it's over. Now you can spend more time at home and maybe we can plan a family vacation," said Faith.

"One thing at a time, honey," he answered. "Right now, let's have a pleasant evening with our friends. It's been too long since we enjoyed spending an evening with another couple.

Faith smiled at Greg. In that moment she felt such a surge of love toward him. She was so happy to be married to him even with all his faults and workaholic tendencies. As they arrived at their friends' house she was thinking that her life was the way she had always dreamed it would be.

"Come in, come in, partner. Congratulations, Ms. Jones, you are the wife of the head of the companies' new marketing department. Next step, president."

"Oh, now, Roger, you're getting a little ahead of yourself, don't you think?"

No, I don't. In fact, I expect this department to become a branch and one of us to be the president. No doubt about it, this can't help but succeed."

I hope you're right, Roger. I intend to do everything in my power to make it happen. My family will be set for life. I have to make this work," Greg said with and intensity that sounded obsessive.

Greg looked at the three of them. They were all staring at him. "My wife would never forgive my being away so much if there wasn't some kind of payoff."

They all laughed but Faith detected a strange reluctance from her friend, Alice. For a few moments she wondered why Alice should be anything but elated. But this really was a special occasion. It was best to keep things light and relaxed, for the first time in months.

"So does that mean you'll stop sending me flowers all the

time, now?" Faith asked.

There was another awkward pause. Faith guessed the men were just exhausted and having the fateful meeting over had left them spent.

"I don't know why he should," Alice said emphatically. "Let's sit down at the table, dinner is ready."

After dinner Greg and Roger started discussing the details of setting up the new department.

"Don't you guys think you could give your wives just one night," Alice said.

"Yes, of course, honey," said Roger.

But in five minutes they were talking about work again. "Oh, we may as well give up, Faith. At least we got to see them tonight. Let's go out on the balcony."

"Okay," Faith said. "I'm just glad it's over. I miss him."

"I'm afraid it just beginning. We have some years of loneliness ahead of us. I know the money will be worth it. But sometimes I wonder if that's enough. I just love that jade jewelry. Where did you get it?"

The evening was pleasant. It was so good to be out together with friends. Eventually the two men found Faith and Alice involved in some conversation about a woman from the club who left her husband for a younger man. They were sorry for the broken family and especially for the children. "I don't know how she could have done that to her family. It's selfish and stupid. He has no education, no money and no prospects. And his family is from a little backwoods' town. She sure had me fooled. I thought she had some sense. Her family won't even talk to her. Even her kids won't see her now. And I don't blame them."

Roger and Greg walked into the room.

"Well, did you run out of thing's to talk about," asked Alice.

"I'm sorry, girls. This is your night, too, we'll try to behave," said Roger.

Greg and Faith exchanged knowing glances. Roger and Alice were dedicated to each other but they had been through some challenges in their marriage. Greg and Faith had talked about it before and were so happy to have avoided the problems most couples have to face.

On the ride home Faith laid her head on Greg's shoulder. "Did you notice that Alice seemed kind of reserved tonight? And did it seem to you that Roger was unusually attentive to her," she asked him.

"Now, Faith, how can you complain about a husband being too attentive," Greg answered with a question.

"It was just an observation, not a complaint. I had a good time. We really have to do this more often."

"I agree," Greg kissed her forehead.

Jason's light was still on when they got home.

"I guess I should have that talk with Jason now," Greg said to Faith.

"I don't know, honey, it's late."

"Putting it off will just make it worse. He'll think he got away with something."

"I guess you're right. Please don't get angry. You don't want an argument before you go to bed."

"I'm not going to argue." Greg knocked softly on Jason's door.

He heard a muffled "Come in" and opened the door.

"Jason, we need to talk about last night. You came in after midnight."

"Yeah, I know dad. We went over to Jeremy's house after the dance and I just lost track of time. Sorry."

"I'm sure you're sorry, son, but there still has to be a consequence."

"What? Don't you think I'm a little too old for a time out? I'll be in college soon and I can do whatever I want."

"That's true and we hope you'll be responsible. But right now, you're still under eighteen and subject to the rules of the house. You know, we make these rules for a reason. You won't be able to drive the car for a week."

"Dad, I already told the guys I'd drive this weekend. We were going into the city for the game."

"I'm sorry, Jason, you'll have to make other arrangements. We can't just dismiss the rules when they're inconvenient. What about your sisters? Do you think I should make exceptions for them, too? When should I stop making exceptions?"

"Why am I responsible for them? I don't understand how any of that applies to me anymore. Don't you trust me? It was only an hour."

"You know it was closer to two hours. And trust doesn't have anything to do with this. Of course we trust you. If we didn't, you wouldn't have as much freedom as you do. Would we let you drive our car if we didn't trust you? But to be given the privileges of an adult you have to at least prove that you can keep track of time. My point is that if we let you slide, we'd have to do the same for your sisters'. You're old enough to understand that it is a parents' responsibility to enforce the rules, regardless of how unjust it seems in this instance. We have to stick to the rules or change them. Would you like Janet to be able to stay out all night? You had to have known that there would be consequences when you saw how late you were. Part of being responsible is accepting the consequences when you make a mistake,"

"Yeah, Okay," said Jason.

In truth Greg wasn't very concerned about it. He knew Jason was sexually active and had provided him with the means and knowledge to protect himself. Boys will be boys, Greg thought. He remembered how he was at that age.

As Greg left the room he was glad he had decided to talk to Jason. He was proud of his son for accepting responsibility for his actions. As far as he was concerned, the matter was closed.

CHAPTER 3

Perspectives

Cindy wanted to be good enough. She wanted to do something so good that her mom would look at her the way she looked at Jason. But no matter how hard she tried she always failed. She got a C on her report card and missed the honor roll. She couldn't even get perfect attendance because she had fallen in gymnastics and hurt her ankle and the doctor had said she should stay off of it for a couple of days. Her parents always said she could do anything if she tried hard enough. And so, she tried. She had worked so hard to win the gymnastics meet that day. She didn't tell anyone about it because she didn't want to be nervous about them watching her. And she didn't want them to see her if she failed.

Mr. Laugherty, her coach, was always helping her. He told her she was limber and had good muscle tone and bone structure for gymnastics. But she knew he had to say stuff like that, he was her coach after all.

"Okay, Cindy, you're as ready as you can be. I know you'll do great today. Why don't you start warming up?"

"Yes, coach."

Cindy started her stretches. I just have to win this meet. I know how proud mom will be, she thought. If I can just be good enough, I might get to the Olympics someday. Well, I might at least get to Nationals. I just have to win this meet. She had been told that worry would work against her but at eight years old she didn't have much control over it. Her need to please her parents motivated her. Her name was called and she moved into position. Her routine was on the balance beam. Her mount was perfect and her moves were good if not quite fluid. But she lost her balance for a split second on her dismount, and it cost her first place.

Mr. Laugherty was ecstatic. He looked at her with such pride and told her what a great job she did. He helped her see what an accomplishment second place was. She qualified for the Statesville meet. She actually did it! Her mother would finally start being proud of her.

Helen was surprised to see so many people when she went to the school to pick Cindy up.

"What's going on here," she asked Cindy.

"We had our competitions today," Cindy was glowing.

"Why didn't you tell us the meet was today? I wish I had been there. How was it?"

"I got second place."

"Oh my gosh, Cindy! That's wonderful! I knew you could do it. You sure worked hard enough"

Cindy was feeling great by the time she got home. She couldn't wait to tell Janet and Jason.

As soon as she saw Janet, she went running up to tell her all about it. But Janet had other things on her mind and just said, "Oh, that's great." Cindy wanted to tell all about it and Janet finally asked her to just find something else to do because she was busy.

Jason came home shortly after and Cindy ran to him and started telling him all about it, but Jason was also distracted. "Cindy, congrats on your blue ribbon, but I'm kind of busy right now."

At eight years old Cindy didn't understand why Janet and Jason bushed her off. But she was persistent in her desire for approval. And she was deflated when she didn't get it.

She waited for her parents to come home and the hours went by in slow motion. Dinner seemed to drag on forever, then shower, putting on pajamas and finally Helen insisted she go to bed. "You can tell them in the morning, honey. You're falling asleep sitting up.'

Even though Cindy told herself that she would stay awake until they go home, exhaustion won out and by the time Greg and Faith got home, Cindy was fast asleep with a little wrinkled brow and her small hands clenched into fists.

In the morning Cindy woke up and dashed downstairs but her parents were already gone. She had been waiting and trying so hard to be patient, like Helen told her to. But Helen said she couldn't even call them. Cindy burst into tears and Helen held her and tried to comfort her. Helen tried to distract her with breakfast and working on her merit badge for Girl Scouts. Cindy made it through another long day of waiting for her parents. She knew that her mom would be so proud of her. Gymnastics was something that her mother was impressed by. She just couldn't wait to see that look of pride in her mother's eyes, the one person she wanted to be proud of her the most.

And then finally her moment came and she heard her mom getting dressed and raced to tell her. The victory wouldn't be complete until she told her mom.

"MOM!" Cindy flew into the room. I won second place at the gymnastics meet yesterday! I had to wait all day to tell you!"

"Oh, that's ok, honey. You'll do better next time," said Faith distractedly.

"But, mom, Mr. Laugherty said I did great. I get to go to the Statesville competition! Can I? Will you and daddy come?"

"When is it," asked Faith.

"It's in September. Can I go?"

"Maybe, honey. We'll have to look at the calendar and I just don't have time right now."

"But, mom, I waited all day. I was practicing patience," cried Cindy. "Can't you just tell me if I can go?"

"Probably, Cindy, but we'll have to wait and see for sure. I didn't even know your meet was yesterday. I'm sorry you didn't win. I know you worked hard for it. You're lucky to have such a good coach. Would you like to help me get ready?"

"I think I'll go back to my room and play games."

"I'll tuck you in before we leave," said Faith.

"Okay." Cindy walked back to her room.

"How could she," she thought. "I worked so hard so she would know I'm good." Cindy turned off her lights, climbed under her blankets and sobbed into her pillow, "How could she, how could she."

Cindy cried herself to sleep that night. It wasn't the first time. She knew now that she could never be good enough. She could never know the acceptance she needed above all else. She was a mistake and unwanted. She knew if she weren't there that her mother would be traveling and Janet and Jason would get to go with her sometimes.

Other people, like her coach and teachers and Helen really seemed to like her. But at home she was just in the way.

Cindy didn't have many friends. She was often depressed going through her day in a kind of dream. And the dream was often a bad one. The one thing that excited her was gymnastics. She was good at it and it was something her mother liked. She had worked so hard for the gymnastics meet and no one was there to see her. She knew that was her fault, she didn't want to hear her parents tell her they couldn't come. And she knew she would be more nervous if her family had been watching. No one knew what she did. And no one seemed to care.

Outwardly Cindy was cute as a button with a dimpled smile and blond curls. She did well in school, was liked by other kids, listened to her teachers and worked hard on gymnastics. She went to Girl Scouts, did her homework and helped Helen.

But inside Cindy was alone. At eight years old she was isolated inside herself behind walls built to keep out the pain of not being good enough. She thought she was letting people down but they just never said it. She was too young to understand it or try to fix it. She was worried and she was scared.

Now she knew there wasn't anything she could do about it. She had tried so hard to be good enough. But she wasn't. And nothing she did could change it. Now her last thread of hope had snapped and left Cindy adrift in a dark world of sorrow.

The bright spot in her life was Helen, she was Cindy's lifeline. It was Helen who was waiting with a snack when she got home from school, Helen who picked her up from practice, Helen who helped with projects and homework, Helen made her supper and often tucked her into bed. Janet was busy with her friends and Jason was at practice a lot. Her parents were always working. Cindy understood the busy lifestyle of her family. But none of that explained the underlying tension which was so tangible it seemed to bounce off the walls. Something was wrong. Cindy could feel it. But she was too young to understand. In her child mind she only knew that she was a disappointment and whatever was wrong was her fault.

CHAPTER 4

Consequences

The weeks flew by apparently unchanged for the Jones household. But it seemed to Helen that the members of this family were drifting further apart. She didn't see them communicating or spending time with each other. And it worried her.

Helen was in the kitchen making dinner and wondering what it might mean.

Cindy was in her room where she had been spending a lot of time lately.

Jason was on the patio by the pool. That was his usual place in the evening for talking on his cell phone.

"Hello."

"Is Jason there?"

"This is Jason."

"Hi, it's Marcia."

"Okay."

"You know, from the Under Twenty-one Night at the club."

"Oh, yeah, how ya doing?"

"I'm pregnant, that's how I'm doing," she blurted out.

"Oh, shit, Marcia. What are you going to do?"

"Jason, it's yours."

"It can't be mine; I used a condom. It's whoever else you were with."

"I wasn't with anyone else, Jason. I've never been with anyone else."

"What? You've got to be kidding. Is this some kind of a joke? Who put you up to this? It can't be mine; I used a condom."

"Jason, this is no joke, believe me. I don't know how it happened. I've heard condoms aren't one hundred percent safe. But I'm sure I'm pregnant."

"Have you seen a doctor?"

"Yes, Carol and I went to family services. I didn't want my parents to know. They tested me and it was positive. Jason, I don't know what to do."

"Carol, you mean my neighbor? Jesus, Marcia. How many people know about this?"

"Carol and I know, of course, and now you. The family services are confidential."

"Can they do a test to find out who the father is?"

"I told you. It has to be yours."

"Well, excuse me for not taking your word for it. I know some girls get pregnant to trap a guy. And I'm sure my parents would want some proof, if we even decide to tell them."

"What do you mean if we decide to tell them? Don't you think they should know that they're going to be grandparents?"

"You're not planning on having it are you?"

"I have no intention of killing my baby. I can't believe you would even say that. We go to the same church. What do you think Pastor David would say?"

"He wouldn't say anything if he didn't know about it. Marcia, we have our lives to think about. We're seniors this year and then we have college. How are you going to do that with a baby?"

"I don't know. I don't know what to do. But, Jason, I know I can't kill this baby. I have to find another way. I have to tell my parents. They know something's wrong. I've been sick in the mornings. I just wanted to tell you first. My parents are going to want to talk to your parents."

"Marcia, wait a minute. Just think about this. Once you tell them there's no going back."

"I have thought about it. And there *is* no going back. I have to tell them. It's the only thing I know for sure. But I'll wait a little if you want. I have to go. Call me tomorrow after school, OK?"

"Yeah, right. See ya."

Jason was stunned. A baby? You've got to be kidding. He couldn't think. He couldn't move. His life was over. He had to convince Marcia to get rid of it. He could convince her. He could convince most girls of anything. He would invite her over and "Hi, Jason." He jumped.

"Carol! You scared the crap out of me."

I just talked to Marica. She asked me to see if you were ok. She knows telling you like she did must have been a shock."

"Ya think?"

"Jason, we've been neighbors for a long time. I like to think that we have a special friendship that's not about football or sex or any of that stuff. I just want you to know that if you need anything I'll be there for you, both of you. She really likes you. It wasn't just a one-night stand for her."

"Yeah, I got that. I don't know what to say."

"You'll be in my prayers tonight."

"Right."

"Jason, you know God is with you and Marcia."

"Well, then He has a sick sense of humor. Why would he try to make me a parent? If He's really there then He knows I'm not ready."

"We can't know the mind of God. Why would you expect to know what His reasons are? He used you to create life inside Marcia. I don't believe He makes mistakes, ya know?"

I'm not sure I do know, Carol. But thanks for coming over. Will you talk to Marcia and tell her I need a few days? Tell her not to do anything, ok? I just need some time. Tell her I'll call her, in a few days.

"Okay Jason, see you later."

As Jason watched Carol go he suddenly had the feeling that he was living someone else's life. This can't be happening, he thought. There's been some kind of mistake.

Jason got up. He couldn't sit still. When he turned around he saw Janet. She was standing there just looking at him.

"I didn't try to hear, Jason. Helen wanted me to get you for dinner. Oh my God, Jason. What are you going to do?"

"I don't know. Just shut up about it, okay?"

"Yeah, okay." Great, Jason thought, four people already knew. But he could trust Janet and Carol. He wondered if they would be able to help him convince Marcia to get an abortion. He couldn't be one of those dead-beat dads who abandoned their kids. But how could he take care of one? He couldn't give up his dreams and get some minimum wage job. He didn't think his parents would be willing to help with a kid. He was nine when Cindy was born. He remembered how hard it was for them. His mom had quit working for a year. She had lost her position at Metropolitan Spa just as she was about to be promoted. No, his mom had worked hard to make up for that year and he wouldn't even ask her to help.

His dad would be furious. Jason remembered the talk they had about being responsible and not letting this happen. His dad would probably side with Jason about the abortion. And Janet... Janet would be on his side no matter what he decided. Carol and Marcia had made their position clear. But if he could just convince Marcia that his way was best, he could pretend this never happened. After all, there was no proof that this was his kid.

As the days went by Jason went through a series of emotions. His life was now a dream with nightmarish qualities. He finally had to admit to himself that he was afraid. He was afraid to tell his parents. Afraid of the anger and disappointment from them that he knew he must face. He was afraid of the future. He no longer had the security of a well laid plan leading to a wonderful life. And he was afraid of being alone. Because he knew that the people who supported him and said they loved him would turn their backs on him when they found out. He would lose the respect of the people that mattered.

At church on Sunday he listened to Pastor David's sermon about living a righteous life and realized that he hadn't been living a righteous life at all, and now everyone would know it. He never really thought about it before but he knew he had sinned and he was afraid. He was afraid of a God with limitless powers who had given His children a specific set of laws and would condemn anyone who refused to live by them. He'd heard it often enough, his choices condemned him. There was no hope, no going back now. Pastor David's sermon interrupted his thoughts.

"We have all sinned and come short of the glory of God. This isn't a house of the righteous but a house of sinners. If you are carrying a heavy burden, come to Jesus. Invite Him into your heart and lay those burdens at His feet. He loves you just as you are, unconditionally. Trust that He will lead you where He wants you to go."

Jason finally understood the words he'd been hearing his whole life. The message was about acceptance despite sin, not condemnation because of it. Christ wants us to be forgiven by the God of the Universe. He wants us to move past our sins and live for love, not focused on sin and evil but focused on goodness and light.

Jason clung to the message of hope. He fought back the tears that threatened during the service and told his parents he had plans so he could stay in the sanctuary afterward. Driven to seek Christ out of the desperate need to be accepted and forgiven, he reached out with his thoughts and his heart.

"Jesus, can you hear me? I know I messed up. I guess I've been messing up for a long time. But Jesus, I don't want to be alone. I don't want to be afraid. Won't you come into my heart? Won't you cleanse me as you promised? I'm sorry for all my sins, Lord. I know I need you to get through this."

As Jason prayed he felt peace envelop him. In some indescribable way he felt love and acceptance. His problem became smaller when faced with the enduring God of the

Universe. The words of Psalm 23 washed over him:

> The Lord is my Shepherd
> I shall not want.
> He makes me lie down in green pastures;
> He leads me beside the still waters.
> He restores my soul;
> He leads me in the paths of righteousness
> For His name's sake.

> Even though I walk through the valley of the shadow of death,
> I will fear no evil;
> For You are with me;
> Your rod and Your staff comfort me.

> You prepare a table before me in the presence of my enemies;
> You anoint my head with oil;
> My cup runs over.
> Surely goodness and mercy shall follow me
> All the days of my life;
> And I will dwell in the house of the Lord
> Forever.

"How can God love me after what I've done? How can he forgive me for messing up so many lives?"

"I often ask myself the same question, Jason."

"Pastor David! I didn't know anyone was here. How did you know what I was thinking?"

"I guess you were thinking out loud. Would you like to be alone?"

Jason told the Minister that he had just accepted Christ. They talked about the difference between believing in God and being born again through Jesus. Then Jason told the minister about Marcia. As he talked about his situation, fear and helplessness crept into his voice.

"What am I going to do?" he said. "I should have never gone out after the dance."

"If your trial has brought you to the Lord, Jason, would you now wish it away? What about the new life which has started? Would you deny the right for that baby to have its own destiny? God has a plan, Jason. You can't see it now, maybe you never will, but we must trust that all is as it should be. And the problems we face in this life will bring us closer to Him if we learn to trust that what happens will ultimately work toward the will of God. Your life will have many problems just as serious as this. But the blessing you will receive from an unplanned pregnancy is obvious when you bring that new life into this world. Jason, you've had the good fortune to have had a life free of crisis so far. Believe me, this isn't the end. This is just the beginning of your life. And it will be filled with happy times as well as hard ones. Learning God's ways and staying in prayer is how we live in His will. I think when you tell your parents, after the shock wears off, everything will be okay.

When Jason left, he noticed how much lighter he felt. He looked at the sky, bright and beautiful and was filled with an inexpressible joy. He could also feel the seeds of doubt, guilt and worry at the edge of his mind. He knew this wasn't going to be easy. He hoped he had the strength to "stay in the light". He wasn't really sure if he understood the meaning but having just come from a dark pit of despair into the light of Christ's love, he had an idea. He was armed better than he knew. God's word had been embedded in his mind since childhood. He would draw on that power in the difficult months and years ahead of him.

Jason had been thinking of Marcia as the person responsible for putting him in this position. In his dark thoughts he had imagined she did it on purpose. She was trying to connect herself with our family, he'd thought. Maybe she just wants to hurt me because I have so much more than she will ever have.

Now he realized that it didn't make any sense for Marcia to put herself through this. She was a smart girl. Of course, she knew she wouldn't get anything but pain from this pregnancy. He wasn't ready to be a father but if what Marcia said about him being the only possibility was true then he was one, ready or not. He realized that he couldn't bear the thought of an abortion any more than Marcia.

It had been four days and he couldn't put off calling her any longer. She sounded like she was crying when he arranged to meet her at the park at 5:00. Of course she's upset. Her life is over too. At least the life they were living now.

Jason had never had a steady girlfriend. He loved to play the field. He had his pick of so many girls. None of them seemed that special. He would go out with them a few times and they would get possessive and brag about being with him. They tried to tell him what to do and where to go. It turned him off and he'd find someone else. He knew they were being hurt and sometimes humiliated. He reasoned they did it to themselves, so it had made sense to him to blame Marcia.

But after he accepted the Holy Spirit into his heart, he saw a different slant on things. Maybe he could have been more considerate. Those girls were people, after all.

He replayed that night of the party in his mind. They were at the Under Twenty-one Night at the Country Club. Marcia was there with another girl. He had never really noticed Marcia before. He knew she was in his class in school, but she was categorized in his mind with things not important in his life.

That night he had been more interested in Barb. She actually looked a lot like a Barbie doll and was often teased about it. She was blond, blue eyed with a gorgeous body. She and Jason had been together before and he knew her to be shallow, fun and good in the sack. Everything he was looking for. He hoped to invite her to the private party later at Jeremys. He prepared to play the game: get her attention, eye contact, and a million-dollar smile. It's just like fishing for girls, he thought. Jason started walking over to her but Ben got there first. Barbie and Ben, Jason thought with a chuckle. Well, it's not like there's a shortage of girls here. Jason veered off to the refreshment table for a drink and to make it look like that was his intention all along. He got his drink, turned quickly and bumped into Marcia. He looked down into the sweetest, clearest blue eyes he'd ever seen. The eyes expanded into a face that showed strength and self-confidence. She excused herself, as he did. She smiled and he thought he saw color rise to her cheeks.

"You're Marcia Griffin, aren't you?"

"Yes, and you're Jason Jones."

"Guilty."

"We have some of the same classes."

"Yeah, I see you around. Didn't you join the choir?"

Jason didn't know why he had wanted to keep the conversation going. But looking back he'd seen the same peace in her face that Carol had. And now he knew that it was the Light of Christ.

Jason wondered how they ended up in bed. Why would something like this happen to her? Didn't Christians have special protection? She said he was her first and he believed her.

She hadn't blamed him or demanded anything when she called to tell him about being pregnant. Of course, she's as scared as I am. She's the one who has a baby started in her body. We both messed up, he realized. We're in this together with God on our side. All he could do was cling to that thought.

When Jason arrived at the park, Marcia was sitting on a bench under a tree. Her once clear eyes were now red and puffy, lines creased her forehead. Her lips were pressed tightly together. But he could still see an underlying calm and knew that peace that surpasses all understanding would be with them now and into an uncertain future.

"Hi," said Jason.

"Hi," she responded.

He sat down; they avoided looking at each other.

"I've been doing a lot of thinking," Jason chuckled a little.

"I don't know how you could laugh at this, Jason. I don't know what I'm going to do."

And now he saw the fear in her eyes. His arms went around

her and she cried into his shoulder.

"I think it's going to be okay, Marcia." Jason didn't know where to begin. Holding her was giving him courage, especially since he didn't have to look into the depths of her eyes.

"I laughed because I really have been thinking about a lot of stuff. I don't know where to begin," he said.

Marcia tried to pull away, but he held her to him and she yielded, consenting to be comforted if only for a few moments.

Jason gently recounted the recent event. Marcia listened to the quiet rumbling voice in his chest. He told her about being overwhelmed and blaming her. How he was planning to try to talk her into an abortion. He felt her stiffen and wetness on his shoulder. "You know, I...I couldn't handle it. I didn't know what to do. I received Christ this morning, Marcia. And I know that he's here with us and everything's going to be okay."

She pulled away and looked at him, her eyes searching for confirmation of truth.

"Some things seem obvious now. First, we are going to be parents. And our parents are going to be upset and disappointed but they're not going to stop loving us. Our lives are going to change but that doesn't mean they can't work out great."

Marcia was stunned. She couldn't believe what she was hearing. She remembered when she was saved. She recognized the joy and love that was coming from him; she could almost see His glow. She saw peace in Jason's eyes, calm resolve and acceptance along with a little fear. "How wonderful! I don't know what to say." And they were once again in each other's arms, this time in a Holy embrace united by Christ.

Marcia had dreaded this meeting with Jason. He'll look at me like an enemy, she had thought. He wants me to have an abortion. She had expected an argument and wasn't prepared for this. She hadn't slept much and had stayed mostly in her room sinking into despair, unable to find the words to pray. She was ashamed and afraid. She had little hope of a positive outcome.

She'd had a crush on Jason since the sixth grade, but he

never really paid much attention to her. He was in sports, and she was in the choir. They saw each other in church and sometimes with their families at the county club. She had let herself be talked into going to the under twenty-one Night with friends and bumped into him, literally. She remembered that night as if it were a dream, her wildest fantasy coming true. She had felt like Cinderella, transformed magically into a princess. She was scared when they went to Jeremy's house but she didn't want the night to end. She's heard that Jason was a good lover and reasoned that he was the kind of guy a girl could trust for her first time. She didn't have any illusions that this would be the start of a true relationship, just a hope that it could lead to something. He was so gentle and loving and they'd fallen asleep in each other's arms. It was a memory she'd treasure forever. She tried not to let the guilt take root. But it had taken its toll in the separation from God that results from unforgiven sin. To her those moments in Jason's arms weren't sinful but loving. She hadn't wanted to cheapen something she had secretly wanted for so long. When she began to suspect she was pregnant, guilt invaded her heart and soul. When three more weeks went by, she got a pregnancy test, then the ordeal with Family Services and finally facing Jason. It had been emotionally traumatic for Marcia. She was caught in a storm that would last the rest of her life. Her phone call to Jason was a nightmare. He wasn't gentle and loving then. He pretty much let her know that she was on her own. After that, until he called her back, she wasn't able to sleep. She imagined he would hate her now. He would try to persuade her to have an abortion. He would turn his back on her. She never imagined that he would be saved and minister to her.

And then in the park he was so gentle and loving again. Just like that night. Her resistance was used up from lack of food and sleep and from the constant worry. She clung to his works of hope and sobbed her pent-up anguish into his chest. He would stand by her and God would be with them. Somehow everything was going to be okay.

"Jason, how are we going to tell our parents?"

LINDA SWANN

CHAPTER 5

Priorities

F aith lived a Christian life. She went to Church. She donated ten percent of her salary, after taxes. She was a dedicated mother and wife. Faith cared about other people and tried not to pass judgement on those that were beneath her.

After Cindy was born she had spent more time in church activities. She had started friendships with some of the women from church who were openly friendly and warm with a true inner glow. Faith had felt so close to God in those days. She had turned to God to fill the emptiness inside, left from the absence of a work routine. Having a baby around again was sweet in a way but Faith needed outside interests besides the gym and she had turned to the church. What had at one time been an obligation became a second family. There was a unity that transcended the superficial relationships she'd had in church before.

Things were so different in those days. Faith had been aware of God's presence. She had felt like a different person, one that was reborn to His love and restoring power someone with hope for a life of service to Him. She had found pleasure in small things, like spending time with the kids and working on their house. She had done a lot of reorganizing and had renovated the kitchen. It was comfortable and she felt great about what she was doing. But sometimes she still missed the challenge of working.

She had heard that the Country Club was hiring a director for their gym. It was a great opportunity and she was hired even though she was older than the other applicants. Her credentials were impeccable; the club was thrilled to get her.

It made her feel so good about herself to be looked up to that way. The Club became her second home and after a few years she was making major changes and improvements. She noticed a change in herself, too. She had a renewed sense of self confidence and control. She threw herself into her work and her personal program to stay looking young.

She knew that her life had changed after Cindy was born. She was determined then to live her life in the will of God. But it was almost impossible with so much focus on her work and herself. Her obligations were at times overwhelming, and Faith loved every minute of it. She thrived on challenge and excelled in her work.

More time spent at the club meant less time with her family and she felt guilty for the time spent away from them. Then she found Helen, who made everything possible.

Faith came to rely strongly on Helen. Helen was a deeply religious woman. It was like having a surrogate mother and minister to help guide them. Faith often had the feeling that Helen was more like the mother of the house, but the commitment to The Club had been made. She was torn between work and home. As the years went by, Faith became comfortable with her routine. Life settled into a pattern. Everything got done, everyone was happy. Sometimes Faith thought about those simple times when Cindy was young. She sensed something missing, but she was too busy to worry about it. She tried to be grateful and not look for things to be unhappy about. Her life was full but in some ways she wasn't as fulfilled as she had been during those blissfully carefree days.

Now Faith got up every morning with a full day ahead of her. She was pushing herself to make up for the time spent having Cindy, determined to do it all. She knew she was a lucky woman. Her children were exceptional, her house was beautiful, her husband was successful and now she would realize her personal goals. It had been difficult at first to be respected as useful in the physically demanding fitness field at her age. But she was beautiful and worked to stay strong and flexible. Her experience proved her to be invaluable. Her position in development allowed her to make changes at the club and provided the challenges that she had so desperately missed. She tried not to feel bad about not being home with her children. She had put her life on hold for her family over and over and now it was her turn. Helen was such a wonderful person and a positive influence on them that she felt they were in good hands.

Today the department head had requested a meeting. She was sure it would be about something positive. Faith had initiated some great classes and hired the instructors. She hoped the meeting was to congratulate her. There was positive feedback on her work, she thought, as she looked through the closet for something to wear. She wanted to look young and professional. She saw something drop and bent down to pick it up.

"A hotel key. Where could it have come from," she thought.

She read the tag, Conquistador 38-B.

"It's those condos on the riverbank, Greg had talked about investing in them. Would he have bought one without even discussing it? I'll find out later. Right now I have to get ready."

Faith looked beautiful in a black skirt, teal silk blouse and a black blazer as she walked into her supervisor's office. "Hi, Janeen," she said.

"Faith, have a seat. I want to congratulate you on the fine job you've been doing. I've had calls from some of our members about our new programs. And your classes are full. We are all excited about the new leagues and competitions. How long do you think it will take to be in full swing?"

"That depends on how many people we have signed up and when they'll be ready. I've been in contact with other country clubs in the county and most are ready to jump right in. I think when they see how well we're doing they'll be knocking on our door to get this started."

"Okay, good," said Janeen. "Do you think someone else will be able to handle it?"

"I don't understand," said Faith.

"I'm sorry," said Janeen. "I've gotten ahead of myself. The board had decided to open a new club overseas. One of the board members knows of an exciting property just outside of a small town in France. The first year will be mostly renovating the property. You will be a consultant and liaison. I know you speak French and with your experience in management and modus operandi here at the club, I can't think of anyone better suited than you.

The second year you would be responsible for implementing some of the same programs we have here and for integrating it into the French community. There is a lot of room for creativity. There I go, getting ahead of myself, again. You'll have to talk it over with your family, of course."

Faith struggled to maintain a professional demeanor. She had heard the rumors of the club in France but she had been so involved with her own projects that she had given it little thought.

"How long would I be away," she asked.

Janeen smiled. "The property will require extensive renovation. Someone else will be in charge of the contractors but we need you there to oversee the project on behalf of the board members. You will be our eyes and ears, seeing the project in terms of functionality and submitting all concerns or changes. We will try for more of a retreat atmosphere. Your programs will have to be modified accordingly. We won't expect things to be running smoothly for several years. There is a three-bedroom cottage on the property that will be yours to use while you're there. Your family would be welcome to live in France during your stay or visit any time. There will be at least monthly opportunities to fly back to the states. And of course a substantial increase in salary. I know the board is hoping you agree. Between you and I, you do have some leverage."

Faith's head was spinning. Her dream was coming true. Surely her family would understand about her needing to go. She would come back to the states every month. She would try to get one week each month at home. She was sure to have a shot at that. France. Oh, my God. Can I really leave my family for that long?

She wondered what impact it would have on her children. And how would Greg be able to handle not having her here. Well, it's not like we've been seeing much of each other lately. It might do him some good to miss me. And then she remembered the condo key. Greg and I have a lot to talk about. I should call him and find some time to just talk. It was still early; maybe he could meet her for a long lunch.

Back in her office she called him. Greg's secretary answered. "Shelia, may I talk to Greg?"

"Sorry, Ms. Jones, he and Amanda are having another meeting and he asked not to be disturbed," Shelia said with a strange emphasis on "meeting."

"It's rather urgent, Shelia, and I won't take but a moment. I'm sure he won't mind. Please ask him for me, will you?" said Faith.

"I'm sure he'll be upset about it. But if you really want me to, I'll ask."

"I'll take all the blame, Shelia. And I just want to ask him to meet me for lunch. I have something important to discuss with him." Faith knew there was an edge to her voice, now.

"Now, Ms. Jones, I know how upset you must be. I can't imagine what you must be feeling. But if I were you, I'd wait until he gets home. Anyway, he already has a lunch meeting scheduled."

"What are you talking about? Upset about what? Shelia, let me talk to Greg, NOW." Faith felt as if she were on a roller coaster poised at the crest of a huge hill. She saw the key, felt the distance between them and what Shelia had just said. It wasn't so much what she said as how she'd said it.

Greg picked up the phone. "Faith, this is a really bad time.

Can I call you back?"

Faith was at a loss for words for the second time that day. "Greg, we really need to talk. Can we meet for lunch today?"

"Today's not good for me," he said.

"You know, I hardly ever ask you to put me first, but this time I have to insist. Something has come up at work. I probably won't get to see you tonight and we really need to talk."

"What is it"

"Meet me at lunch at Lombardo's."

"Okay, I'm not sure how long I'll be able to stay."

"Fine"

"You okay?"

"Not really. No, I'm not okay. I'll see you at lunch. Go back to your "meeting."

"All right, I'll see you then, honey."

Faith wanted to scream. Her husband was having an affair. She had wondered from time to time when he seemed distant and distracted. She always thought it was his dedication to his job. But now she was seeing clearly. The awkward pauses in conversation at dinner with Alice and Roger months ago had stuck in her mind. All those late nights and the times he didn't come home at all. He said he slept in the office. Then she remembered the key from this morning. Shelia's strange voice when she said "meeting" and her comment about what Faith must be feeling. Oh, God, Alice knows and Shelia. She was spinning out of control. She had to put France and Greg out of her mind. She had work to do. She would deal with the rest in a couple of hours at lunch.

Faith arrived at Lombardo's before her husband. She sat at the table awaiting a confrontation she wasn't prepared for. The clatter of silverware, the waiter taking an order and the conversations around her all made her painfully aware that she and Greg wouldn't be alone. Everyone looked so normal, happily eating and talking as if this were just any day. "How could I have been so blind?" she thought. And then "Maybe I'm jumping to the wrong conclusion." She waited anxiously, desperately hoping her husband would prove her suspicions wrong.

She watched him walk in, then. He was so handsome, she loved him so much.

"Faith," Greg leaned over and brushed her lips with his. Faith recoiled. It was a reflex, but in that instant Greg suspected that his affair wasn't a secret anymore. "What's going on?"

"You're asking me?" she said.

"You said there was something going on at work."

Was he trying to bait her? No, after almost 20 years of marriage, Faith knew by looking at him that he was just asking about her work. Could he be more insensitive?

"I know about your affair, Greg. It's Amanda, isn't it," Faith couldn't stop herself from saying it.

"Faith, you know how much I love you," Greg started.

"Oh, God," her hand flew to her mouth. "You have a poor way of showing it. Don't say anything else. Look, I was offered a chance to go to France to direct the opening of a spa there and I think I should go. I'll talk to Helen about her moving into the maids room while I'm gone. With us both getting raises I'm sure we can make it worthwhile for her," she said.

"What are you talking about? You can't just go off to France and leave your family. You have obligations here."

Faith fumed, "Don't talk to me about obligations. In fact don't talk to me at all. Our conversation is over. Please don't come home tonight."

"Where do you expect me to go?" he asked.

Right now, Greg, I really don't care. Sleep in your office, again. Or sleep at the Conquistador, although you'll have a hard time getting in without your key." Faith ran out of the restaurant.

Faith called Janeen and told her that she had a lot of thinking to do and she couldn't get much work done that afternoon, (all true, she told herself) and took the rest of the day off.

Helen was there when she got home. "Are you okay," she asked.

"Yes, everything's okay, Helen. I'm just not feeling up to par today and my work is at an impasse. I thought I'd just come home early and rest this afternoon. Unless you have some project started you may as well go home, too. I'll be here for the kids today and take care of dinner. Do any of them need picked up today?" "No, Jason has a ride after practice. Janet and some of her friends are going to the mall and Ms. Penske will drive them today. Cindy doesn't have practice today and should be home on the bus. I was just going to start dinner. Are you sure you don't want me to make anything?"

"No, Helen, I think I'll treat the kids to pizza tonight."

"All right, Faith, if you're sure. I'll see you tomorrow. Are you sure you're okay?"

"I'm fine," Faith sighed. "I'm going to do some laps before the kids get home."

"Well, call if you need anything," Helen said. "Have a good evening."

Helen knew something was terribly wrong but there wasn't anything she could do about it until Faith told her what it was. She got her bag and left the house wishing she could do something to help.

The water was heated but the air was cool as Faith dove into the pool. She needed to move and so she swam until she was physically spent. Then she cried until she drained her emotions. By the time the kids came home she had gained some control of herself. She was going to France. She thought about taking the kids but she knew that taking them from familiar surroundings and then not being able to spend time with them wouldn't be best for them. They could come over and spend the summer next year. But this decision would be what was best for her. She no longer cared what Greg wanted and the kids were busy with their own lives.

She would wait a couple of weeks until the plans were more concrete. Then she would tell them. Until then, Greg apparently had an apartment. He could stay there. Chances are the kids wouldn't even know that he wasn't coming home to sleep. When she thought about it that's all he had been doing at home for a long time now. Why had he sent those beautiful bouquets which had filled her with such love? Did he feel guilty or was he just trying to manipulate? Faith felt so stupid, humiliated, and afraid of an uncertain future.

CHAPTER 6

Choices

Greg Jones lived the "American dream." His children were well adjusted and did well in school. Greg had everything a man would want, a nice house, a beautiful family, a great job with a good future. He was a good provider and loving husband and father. But no matter what he achieved it was never completely fulfilling. He never quite put his finger on what was missing. He convinced himself that having a mistress would calm his restlessness, and it did, for a while. He wasn't exactly cheating, he reasoned. He was making a happy home. He didn't love the women he slept with, not like he loved his wife and family. He kept them around until they became a nuisance or boring.

His first mistress, after twelve years of marriage, seemed to put the spring back in his step. His mundane existence became bright again. His whole family responded by being happier. Instead of wanting to spend time away from home, he found himself looking forward to being with his family. The affairs never lasted long. The mistress would realize his devotion to his wife and family and know there was no future in a relationship with him.

Greg had repeated the same scenario several times, now. His latest was Amanda. He knew it was risky to have an affair with someone in the office but he was drawn to her and it was easy to plan their meetings.

When Roger accidently witnessed Greg and Amanda embracing, Greg explained it away by flirting gone too far. Then at the congratulation dinner he suspected that Roger had told Alice what he had seen and hadn't believed Gregs' explanation. It also wasn't surprising that Shelia, his secretary would have noticed the long meetings and knowing looks between Amanda and himself. Greg stayed too busy to spend much time thinking about it until the day when his wife called to invite him to lunch.

Greg went through a series of thoughts and emotions. My God, she knows, he thought. There's no proof that she knows. Maybe he was just jumping to conclusions. It was probably like she said, something important happening at her work. Why worry about something he wasn't even sure was a problem. After all, if he was happy and fulfilled he would be a better husband and father, he told himself again.

He loved his wife but right now he was playing with Amanda and he turned his attention back to her. Amanda was young and soft. He pulled her into his lap and nuzzled her neck, breathing deeply to fill his senses with her scent.

"What's going on," she asked.

"I have to meet Faith for lunch, sorry, we can go later or just wait until tomorrow."

"Oh, Greg, I've been looking forward to going out in public with you. We hardly ever do anything except go to the condo."

"Yes, but we have so much fun there." His hands on her body made her forget to complain. Her response to his touch was what he desired as he looked at the clock to see how much time he had to play with Amanda before he had to meet Faith for lunch.

"Faith," Greg leaned over and brushed her lips with his. Faith recoiled. It was a reflex, but in that instant Greg suspected that his affair wasn't a secret anymore. "What's going on," Greg put on his poker face.

"You're asking me?" she said.

"You said there was something going on at work."

"I know about your affair, Greg. It's Amanda, isn't it," Faith was never one to hold back what she was thinking.

"Faith, you know how much I love you," Greg started.

"Oh, God, you have a poor way of showing it. Don't say anything else. Look, I was offered a chance to go to France to direct the opening of a spa there and I think I should go. I'll talk to Helen about her moving into the maids room while I'm gone. With us both getting raises I'm sure we can make it worthwhile for her," she said.

"What are you talking about? You can't just go off to France and leave your family. You have obligations here."

Faith fumed, "Don't talk to me about obligations. In fact don't talk to me at all. Our conversation is over. Please don't come home tonight."

"Where do you expect me to go?" he asked.

Right now, Greg, I really don't care. Sleep in your office, again. Or sleep at the Conquistador, although you'll have a hard time getting in without your key." Faith ran out of the restaurant.

After all the time they had been together and now just when life was getting comfortable, he had to deal with this. Greg remained angry and defensive for the rest of the workday. He and Amanda picked up Japanese take-out and took it to the condo. Amanda was glad about the turn of events. She assumed Greg would feel closer to her. But instead he seemed distant and Amanda decided to give him some space. "He will need time to come to terms with the break-up, she thought. She went home and Greg was left with his own thoughts.

Disappointment was an alien feeling for Greg. He was always in control. When he wanted something, he got it. When there was a problem, he fixed it. But he knew his wife and wondered if he would be able to fix this. The next day at work he had trouble concentrating. He didn't want to be with Amanda, didn't want to be at the condo. But when repeated attempts to contact Faith failed, he figured going home wasn't an option right away. He had his secretary send her a dozen roses.

"This is damn inconvenient," Greg thought. "Everything

was fine when she didn't know about Amanda. She could have just looked the other way. What was the big deal, anyway? They don't mean anything to me. It's just entertainment."

Six weeks passed and still Faith wouldn't talk to him. He'd gone to the house where everything seemed normal but Faith wasn't there. He called The Club and left messages but she didn't call back or answer her cell.

The holidays were coming up and he was alone. "What right does Faith have to kick me out of my house and keep me from seeing my own children." He thought.

Greg never really considered getting a divorce. This was just another problem to be dealt with. But how could he fix it when Faith wouldn't listen to his explanations? He'd left a message on her cell and tried to tell her that he didn't have feeling for Amanda. He didn't bring up any other women from the past. She would definitely lose it if she knew. Apparently Faith didn't care about his point of view. She was just mad and wanted retribution for her hurt feelings. So she kicked him out to make him suffer. Greg felt he had suffered enough. I'm going to start spending more time at home whether Faith likes it or not. She'll get used to the idea. I'll be home for the holidays. Greg had no intentions of spending Christmas alone. He belonged with his family; in the home he had worked so hard to provide for them.

He called the kids to talk to them whenever he could. He probably talked more to them now then he had in years. They seemed to be okay. Faith had told them that she needed some "space." Jason took it in stride. Cindy was too young to understand and nothing much had changed in her life because her dad wasn't sleeping at home. It was sad to realize that she didn't really notice his absence. Greg thought Janet knew there was a problem between her parents. She didn't seem too concerned about it. He supposed that she knew, as he did, that they would work it out.

CHAPTER 7

Comfort

Janet felt like her life was over, her family was torn apart. Her bother was going to be a father. Her parents were going to get divorced because her father was having an affair. Her mother may be going to France, leaving them at a time like this. Cindy was isolated, staying mostly in her room.

School had started and Janet's friends didn't come over much anymore. Their parents had heard about her dad having an affair and didn't want them involved. How could he do this? She knew how hurt her mother was. Janet heard her crying sometimes when she thought she was alone.

Janet wanted to leave this house and all the unhappiness. She couldn't bear the thought of spending a Saturday night here. She sat in front of the TV but couldn't find anything interesting to watch. She walked out to the pool and watched the water bubbling up from the pump. The gurgling sound only emphasized the quiet. She went into the kitchen where Helen was starting dinner. The smell of food turned her stomach. But at least Helen was there. Janet was thankful for Helen. She was an island in the storm. Only Helen seemed to offer any comfort.

"Helen, please let me come and spend the night with you. I just need to get away from here for a little while."

"Honey, I can't leave Cindy by herself and Jason may not be

back for a long time."

"We can take her, too. It would be good for her. She spends all her time in her room."

"But, Janet, I'm going to church tonight."

"Please, Helen. We'll go with you. We'll be good. We don't take up much room. Please."

"Let me call your mom."

"She'll say it's okay. She'll be glad to have us out of the way for the night."

"Now, Janet, you know your mom loves you. You will survive this. And even though I know it doesn't help to hear it, you will be stronger for having lived through it."

"You're right. It doesn't help."

Faith easily gave permission; she really did sound kind of relieved. Helen put away the ingredients for cooking and helped the girls get ready for their outing.

Helen and the girls drove to the other side of town. They went to a fast-food restaurant, a special treat for them. Janet, of course, picked at a side salad. They ate in silence then went straight to the church. Pastor Simon was starting his new series of sermons on God's Grace.

Let us pray. Janet was shocked to hear "The Jones Family" mentioned in the prayer requests. She looked at Helen who reached over and squeezed her hand. "It was all I knew to do." Janet saw the love and caring in Helen's eyes. She clung to that look. It seemed like a long time since Janet had felt warmth like that.

"For God so loved the world that He gave His only begotten Son that whoever believes in Him shall not perish but have everlasting life. Sons and daughters of God, these aren't just words."

Helen glanced at the girls. Cindy was staring at her hands in her lap. She looked detached from the surroundings. Janet was listening. Pastor Simon explained the basis of the Christian faith and how walking with Christ, while it doesn't stop life from handing you difficulties, it does help you bear them through the power of the Holy Spirit. And even when you turn from God, He is still with you. He loves you and is waiting for you to talk to him and to be with Him. Tears were flowing freely down Janet's cheeks. Will you receive Christ today? Will you let Him into your heart? Let Him heal you and comfort you? Janet looked like she would like to go up but was afraid. When the man behind her walked up the aisle, she followed.

It was so unexpected. Helen remembered her own joy at the moment she received Christ. Cindy was staring open mouthed. "You can't let her do that," she whispered. "She'll be a fanatic. Mommy and Daddy won't like it."

"This is between God and Janet, Cindy. Don't worry; everything is going to be okay."

Janet's face was glowing with the others who had received Christ that night. They hugged each other and then she came back to Helen and hugged her and Cindy.

Janet had never known such profound love. She knew in that moment that she was changed.

After the service they went back to Helen's apartment. They put Cindy to bed in the spare room and she and Janet sat up and talked far into the night. They talked about what had happened and about the power of prayer. They talked about the Bible, about Christ's sacrifice. Janet had so many questions. Helen explained that although she had changed, her circumstances hadn't and neither had Janet's family. There wasn't anything Janet could do about them but to love and support them. Only God could help and Janet's part was to pray and have faith. "It may be hard in the days ahead but I'll be there to help. And we can pray together."

"Do you want to pray now," Helen said.

"Yes."

"Dear Lord, thank you for our new sister. Help her to walk in your Grace as she faces the trials ahead. Help her to know that everything is according to your plan and to believe everything will be okay, Lord. Be with her family during these difficult times. Please lead them to know you, that they may also do your will. In Jesus name, Amen."

"It's time for bed, honey. Do you want to sleep with Cindy in the spare room?"

"I'll be okay here. I just want to spend some time alone with Him."

"I know just how you feel, Janet. Good night. I'll see you in the morning."

It was so exciting to be here with Janet tonight. Helen thanked God, again, for Janet and for all the Jones family. His blessings never stopped and came so often through them even at a time like this.

In the morning Janet was looking forward to going home, which surprised Helen. And then she realized that Janet, as a new Christian, was ready to spread her wings and make some changes. In jeans and a tee shirt, she reminded Helen of her own children at that age. They had all eventually found their way to Christ.

Janet had her whole life ahead of her. Helen was happy to be here to help with her first tentative steps. They read James 1:2-5, "My brethren, count it all joy when you fall into various trials, knowing that the testing of your faith produces patience. But let patience have its perfect work, that you may be perfect and complete, lacking nothing. If any of you lacks wisdom, let him ask of God who gives to all liberally and without reproach, and it will be given to him."

"You know, none of this made any sense before, but it makes sense now."

"That's the Holy Spirit in you, Janet. It's important to read your Bible every day. That's how we learn His wisdom. Do you have a Bible?"

"Yeah, we each got one in our youth group at our church. Helen, why didn't I ever accept Christ at our church?"

We are led to accept God in His time, honey. We can't know the mind of God. That's what it says in the Bible. Sometimes we turn to Him during tough times. He was always there loving us but we only turn to Him out of our own need. And that's okay because now that you know Him, you will never be the same."

Faith was there when they got home. "Ms. Jones, are you okay? What are you doing home?"

Girls, go up and get your shower and change. Cindy and Janet went up the stairs, each wondering what was going on. Faith barely noticed them these days, it seemed Janet wondered if her mom had heard what happened last night. But how could she know? Well, she would trust in God as Helen did. Things couldn't get much worse around there.

"Helen, we've known each other for a long time. I'm sure you've heard some of what's going on here. I don't know how things got so out of control and I don't even know where to start. One of the girls Jason went out with has gotten pregnant and claims Jason is the father. He hasn't denied it so I guess it's possible. I shouldn't be surprised when his own father is having an affair with someone at his office. He bought a condo to have a place to go with her. That's where he's been staying.

The Country Club has decided to purchase a property in France and has asked me to go and oversee the opening of a new club there. This is exactly what I've always wanted to do. At first it seemed like a bad time to be thinking about working so far from home but the more I think about it the more I realize that the timing may be perfect for me. Maybe it's time I do something for myself. I've always done what Greg wanted and now I don't care what he wants. This is my chance and I want to take it. And that's where you come in. I want you to move in here and take care of the kids while I'm gone. I'm asking you to do this so they won't have to move or change schools. It would be the best thing for them. I know you said you don't want to live here and I respect that. I would be willing to pay your rent at your apartment along with a substantial raise while you stay here. That way it would be there for you when I get back. Just think about it, will you? I'm going one way or the other. I just think this would be best for the kids."

Helen was thinking about it. She was thinking that this definitely was not the best thing for the kids.

"I'll need some time to think and pray. Are you sure about

this?"

"It's the chance of a lifetime for me, Helen. I put my career on hold for my children and my husband. The kids are mostly grown and doing their own thing now and my loyalty to my husband was apparently misplaced. I know Jason has a bumpy road ahead. He made an adult choice and will have to face the adult consequences. I won't throw him out of this house, but I won't take care of his problem for him, either. I haven't given my answer, yet, at work. But, yes, I'm leaning toward going."

"While we're talking I feel I should tell you that Janet accepted Christ at church last night."

"That's good. Maybe she will rejoin the youth group. I'd hate to see her go through what Jason and that girl, I don't remember her name, is going through.. Abortions are such ugly things."

"They're having an abortion?"

"I certainly hope so. They're obviously too young to have a baby. Who would take care of it?"

CHAPTER 8

Changes

With the change of seasons came changes in the lives of the Jones Family. Helen had worked for the Jones for years. She'd seen them go through crises of daily living. Cindy had low self-esteem, Janet's rather promiscuous way were natural innocent adolescent behavior, she thought. Jason was self-important, a teenage idol. Greg and Faith were warm, wonderful people with a tendency toward being workaholics. Helen knew them and accepted the human traits of a good family. Now the atmosphere was charged. A storm was coming. There were no open confrontations that she could see, but the household was cold and strained. Helen believed that God had led her to this family. Her only witness was to let them know she was born again, and love them unconditionally, as Christ teaches.

Helen preferred to see the "sunny side of life." She did all she could to bring peace to this household. She gave her love and caring generously. She was kind and attentive. She prayed God would help heal the problems. She had added the Jones family to the prayer list at church. She helped and encouraged. But Helen knew she couldn't tell this family how to live or fix the issues they had to face. And Helen knew that it is through trials and suffering that we mature and grow.

The Jones believed in God and went to church but she

knew they weren't truly committed to living in Gods will. Helen didn't judge them; she accepted them and loved them. What do you do when someone you care about is doing something self-destructive? You can't council them and you can't help them unless they want you to. All you can do is give it to Jesus knowing that He has a plan for His Children. You love them, listen and sympathize.

Each member of this family was deep into their own lives. Jason was usually away from home. Helen wanted very much to tell him that even though he was too young to become a father, it didn't mean this tiny being shouldn't have the chance at life. She couldn't know his thoughts were the same. Helen loved the young man and the unformed child he had helped to conceive. She already felt as if there were another member of this family. The thought of destroying it crushed her. Yet she had no right to even argue her point. She had felt like a part of this family for a long time. Now she was separated from them. And there wasn't anything she could do except pray.

Cindy tried to stay in her room most of the time. She had lost interest in gymnastics. Her coach had stopped by to talk to Greg and Faith but they were both at work. He told Helen that Cindy's enthusiasm was gone and she wasn't progressing. Helen told the coach that she had noticed it at home, too.

"This happens sometimes," he said. "I'll work with her at practice. I wouldn't worry too much about it but don't let her quit. She needs something she is good at to get her through rough patches, even if she spends part of her practice watching. Just being there is good for her if she's battling depression.

Helen realized that's exactly what was going on. She needed to get Cindy talking.

Helen and Cindy were alone in the house after school often. One day Helen distracted Cindy from going up to her room by baking cookies. The smell of cinnamon and vanilla brought warm thoughts of Christmas. They chatted as they dropped dough onto the cookie sheet. They talked about school and gymnastics. Cindy seemed unusually receptive to conversation so Helen took the opportunity to discuss Janet's decision to give her life to Christ.

"Did you notice how much happier your sister is since she accepted Jesus?"

"I guess so. I don't understand why she would want to be fanatic," Cindy said.

Helen knew where she had gotten that idea. "Janet didn't become "fanatic', Cindy. She just told Jesus she was sorry for anything she did wrong and promised to try harder. Have you noticed her trying harder?"

"Yes, I think so. Why did she cry if that's all it was?"

"Honey, when you talk to Jesus like he's standing there, right in front of you looking right into your heart and you've been missing Him so much for a long time, it just makes you want to cry for joy."

"I hardly see anyone anymore. Janet smiles a lot but when I see her she hardly even says hi. She doesn't even tell me to leave her alone anymore."

"I think she has a lot going on. Everybody does. Your family loves you, Cindy. I think Janet, Jason and your parents are just trying to protect you from adult stuff that you shouldn't have to worry about at your age."

"I know what's going on. I can hear them talking on the phone and when they don't know I'm listening. Mommy is going away. She doesn't love daddy and us anymore. And Jason's friend Marcia is going to have a baby. He's real upset about it. Janet's telling all her friends about Jesus and some of them don't like her anymore. And no one even cares about me, except you and coach."

"I'm sure it must seem that way sometimes. The truth is that your parents love you very much. They're having some troubles right now. But, Cindy, all families go through hard times and they get past it. The Bible says that God uses trials to make a perfect work in us. That means we learn from our troubles. Some people turn to God for help like Janet did. Some people learn lessons like how nice it is when everyone gets along."

Cindy looked up at Helen with tears in her eyes. "I wish things could go back to the way they were."

"I know, little one. Things will get better. Would you like to ask God to help?"

"I don't want to do what Janet did."

"No, honey, we'll just ask God to help. Dear Lord, please be with this family in their time of trial. We know that this is how we learn to do what you want us to and how to be grateful for what we have. Be with Cindy, Lord. Help her know that her family needs her just as much as she needs them. In Jesus name we pray, Amen."

Janet came in as the first batch of cookies was coming out of the oven. "Mmm, that smells good. What kind are they?"

"Oatmeal, raisin, chocolate chip. We went all the way. Would you like one?" Janet's appetite had improved lately. It wasn't any drastic change, just a notable improvement Helen thought Janet had been eating more meals and occasionally even a snack.

Helen remembered years ago when she had accepted Christ and stopped trying to control everything and everyone around her. That was just before she had started working for the Jones. She remembered the freedom she felt after she handed the reins to Christ. She was no longer responsible for making everything perfect or making others happy. She needed to learn to trust that God was taking care of things. She didn't have the answers and her part was to learn Gods will. So she found a church family and studied the Bible. She learned how to walk in the Grace of God. She knew now that she was setting up a pattern of learning for her life and that graduation comes at the end of life on earth.

But Janet was new. She was on fire for Christ. She wanted everyone she cared about to feel as good as she did. She had a passion to learn more about being a Christian, and the Bible, particularly the written words of Jesus from the Gospels. She thought it was beyond amazing that she could read the actual words of Christ.

She had joined the youth group again and participated in all their functions. Helen thought she could almost feel Jesus' presence when Janet was in the room. Janet thought that Helen was the one person in this household who understood and approved of her newfound faith.

The three sat comfortably in the kitchen munching on warm cookies and drinking cold milk. Helen and Janet were talking about some of the things the youth group was doing when Cindy got up and started toward the door.

"Cindy, where are you going," asked Helen.

"I'm tired," said Cindy. "I'm going up to my room."

"I'm worried about your sister," Helen said after Cindy left the room. "I talked to her today and I know it helped her but she could really use your love and support. She thinks no one in this family loves her or cares about her. She feels all alone."

"I've noticed her spending lots of time in her room. But she always does that," said Janet. I don't know what I can do. Is she too young to get saved? Jesus could help her."

"Part of our work as a Christian is to help others. God works through us. Pray about it, Janet. Chances are Jesus will tell you what He wants you to do."

"I have prayed. I've asked and asked. How will I know if He is talking to me?"

"When Jesus speaks to us there are no other thoughts in our mind, only his word. And they will be a still, small voice. God also speaks to us through the Bible. We learn how we should be living our Christian life. The longer we walk with God through prayer and reading our Bibles, the easier it will be to know His will."

Helen felt honored and privileged to be a part of Janet's new Christian walk. It was amazing to watch her priorities change, become less self-centered and worldly. Instead of spending her time primping and lounging with friends, Janet was spending time with the youth group, learning and helping others. Janet still had impeccable taste in her clothes and makeup. But that wasn't her priority anymore. She looked more at ease with herself, not like she was trying to impress with her looks.

Jason came in later and Helen offered him a cookie. Cindy had gone into the living room and turned on the TV. Helen considered it an improvement over retreating to her bedroom. Janet was watching a classic children's movie with her. Jason went in and watched, too. Helen brought some cookies in the den and sat down and watched. It was a story about some animals that were lost and trying to find their way home. How ironic, she was sure they could all identify.

Helen was watching the children as closely as the movie. They laughed together at the funny antics of the animals. It was amazing the three Jones kids wearing the same expression during the suspenseful parts. Jason teased Janet and Helen for crying about a happy ending. Cindy was just looking at them as if she suddenly understood something. Helen could almost see a light bulb over her head like in the old comics.

Faith came in while they were talking. She took the opportunity to explain to them the plan that would allow her to be home one week out of the month and summer vacation would be in France. While they were excited about spending the summer in France, they voiced concerns about missing their friends, parties and all of the summer activities they looked forward to. Faith knew they could work out the details. It was just nice to be talking about it.

"What about dad?" asked Jason.

"Apparently your dad bought a condo and has decided to stay there for a while."

"Are you getting a divorce?"

"Nothing has been said about a divorce. But your dad and I have some things to work out."

"How will you do that if he's living in a condo and you're in France?"

"That's a question that doesn't have an answer yet."

"He left because you're going to France, didn't he?"

"It's hard to explain. I don't even understand all of it myself. But everything will work out, you'll see. And I want you to come and talk to me anytime you want to. I won't be leaving until after Christmas, and like I said, I'll be coming home all the time. Helen will be living here instead of her apartment while I'm gone. Faith gave Helen a grateful smile.

"You'll be able to go to your schools and you'll have your friends." Faith shot an accusing look at Jason.

"What," he said.

"I guess you and I need to sit down and have a serious talk."

"Yeah, we do need to talk. I've been waiting for the right time to tell you this. I...well, I...accepted Christ," Jason stuttered.

No one said anything. The ticking clock, which no one had even noticed, now seemed to echo in the stillness.

Then Janet said," Oh my God, Jason, I did, too."

Janet and Jason reached for each other and embraced in a true spirit of siblings, not only by birth but now also joined by the Holy Spirit. "Oh, Jason, isn't it great? Why didn't you tell me? How did it happen for you?"

Jason told his story and they all cried, except Cindy. She understood, now, that these were tears of joy and she had a deep sense of the rightness of it. She was inadvertently experiencing the profound love of Christ through her brother and sister.

Janet glowed as she gave her testimony to her family. The Lord filled the room and their hearts. Everyone was quiet as she told them about the joy she felt at the moment she accepted Christ. She talked about some of the problems she'd had since then.

Janet's newfound faith had changed her life. She now knew the peace of the love of God. She really did want to shout it from the mountain tops. She wanted to tell everyone. She craved His word. There wasn't any doubt, she had changed. With the unabashed enthusiasm of a teenager, Janet started telling her friends about her life changing experience. Not everyone was happy for her. It was difficult for her to understand why some of her friends, especially the ones who went to her church, would look right through her now, when they passed in the hall at school. They all listened to the same sermon on Sunday, why couldn't they understand? And why were they avoiding her?

She was determined to live up to her decision to follow

Christ, accepting that some of her friends wouldn't want to be around her anymore. But she didn't realize that her whole world was about to change. The kids she knew from youth group became her new peer group. She wasn't one of the "popular girls" anymore, a station she had always enjoyed. The loss seemed small to her compared to what she had gained. Her new friends were less petty, the friendships more meaningful. It wasn't long ago she was laughing at "those fanatics." Now she saw a different perspective. That realization also helped Janet understand that everyone has their own perspective that is subject to change.

Janet and Helen had become closer. Janet often turned to Helen to talk about personal things. Faith didn't share Janet's perspective so it was hard to make her understand what the issues were. Although Faith was physically present and emotionally supportive, she was so distracted that sometimes it seemed to Janet that her mom was not really there.

"I don't feel right about trying to get guys to look at me like I used to, especially after what's happening to Jason. A lot of my friends don't understand when I try to tell them how Jesus can change their life, too. They look at me like I'm crazy and say they don't want to change."

"We come to the Lord in His timing," said Helen.

"I'm so happy for you, Janet," said Faith. "You look radiant. Have you thought about joining the youth group at church?"

"I already did, mom. I've been thinking about going to Helen's church, though. That's where I was saved. There aren't as many people there and they all seem to know each other. I think everyone hugged me that night. They like me there."

"I'm sure they do, honey. But all our friends go to the one down the street and you can walk or ride your bike there."

"I'll think about it, mom. It is nice to be able to go to Bible study and stuff without having to get a ride."

Helen wisely decided to keep her opinions to herself. She was happy to be included in this private family moment since she'd be moving in and helping these children cope with the trials ahead. Ultimately going to church and having Christian support was the most important thing.

"This is so nice, all of us together. How about making family night tradition once a week until I go? They all agreed and decided on a night."

Each of them felt the moment was precious. Each also felt the absence of Greg.

Cindy curled up in Faith's lap. While she couldn't understand most of what was being said, she could sense the peace and love present in the room. They were a family and that didn't change. As they went to bed, each with their own thoughts, they felt closer than they had in a long time.

Faith lay in bed thinking about Jason and Marcia, the girl he got pregnant. She knew she would have to talk to the girl's parents soon. She didn't know what she would say or do but she knew that avoiding the problem would likely cause more problems.

The next day Faith called Meg Griffin, Marcia's mother.

"Hi, Meg, it's Faith, Jason's mom."

"I know who you are, what can I do for you?"

"I feel strange calling you like this, but I wondered what you had decided to do about Marcia's pregnancy. Jason said she's planning on having the baby."

"You know, Mrs. Jones, I haven't heard from you in all this time. I don't even see you except at church and you barely acknowledge us. Then you call me up out of the blue and want to know what <u>we</u> plan to do about <u>Marcia's</u> baby? Did you know she'll be finishing high school in virtual school? We're trying to keep this thing quiet. Personally, Mrs. Jones, I think Jason should step up to the plate. They've started a family. They should do it together."

"I can understand why you would say that. In a perfect world they would get married and live happily ever after. But neither of them is old enough to care for the needs of a baby. They're not even old enough to care for their own needs. They still have to go to college to be able to provide for a family, and that's just the financial needs. We both know there's a lot more to raising kids than money.

"It would be hard but they're both intelligent people. I've noticed that they obviously have strong feelings for each other. I'm curious, Mrs. Jones, why did you wait so long to call me?"

"It was my understanding that Marcia would be having an abortion. I'm glad she's not and I'm glad we're talking, now. Why don't we meet for lunch?"

"I'd like that, Mrs. Jones."

"And call me Faith. It'll be my treat. That way I can apologize for any insensitivity on my part and we can get better acquainted."

"Okay, Faith, I'd like that."

"Lombardo's at noon?"

"See you there. I'm glad to have you on board. I'm looking forward to talking to you," said Meg.

Over lunch Meg and Faith discussed their kid's situation. Meg thought a child needed both parents and a stable home. Faith thought that the kids were too young to understand what a marriage commitment meant. Meg thought that the pregnancy meant they needed to go out and start their own lives. Faith felt that they should have help until they finish college. Faith wanted to give them a shower, Meg wanted to keep it quiet. It wasn't an argument, just an exchange of opinions. In the end they both agreed it was Marcia and Jason's decision. It was way past time for all of them to sit down and talk. They decided to wait until after Thanksgiving. Meg told Marcia, Faith told Jason and within an hour the two young parents were on the phone discussing the new development.

Okay, honey, here we go. This is our chance to tell them what _we_ want to do," said Jason. "I'm not sure they will listen to us, anyway. My parents are really mad. We have to decide what's best for the baby."

"Okay, Jason. Bye."

"Good night, honey."

Jason had started using affectionate names when talking to her. He had never done that before but then he had never felt like this about a girl before. He sat down on the lounge chair by the pool and tried to will his muscles to relax. The breeze was chilly that night, a foreshadowing of fall. But all Jason could think about was Marcia, and his baby.

Thanksgiving was only weeks away and they would have to have a plan by then.

CHAPTER 9

Absent

It was late when Greg got to the condo on the night before Thanksgiving. He thought again about how much he missed going home at night. Here he was living in this place he had bought as an investment "and to cheat on my wife." He didn't want to hear his conscience but there it was.

Greg had been angry when he first moved out. Then his conscience began to nag at him. "You broke your vows, betrayed your marriage. How would you feel if Faith had lovers?" Greg's conscience was a nuisance. He poured himself a scotch.

Amanda had stopped coming over. They'd had so much fun together at first. Now his interest in her had waned. She expected him to turn his back on his family and start a life with her. When she realized that Greg had no intention of marrying her, she found someone else. It was no great loss to Greg. The truth was that he wasn't having a good time with her anymore, he admitted to himself. She had proven to be much more trouble than she was worth.

Greg drank to feel better but the loneliness only became more noticeable. The scotch wasn't working but he poured another drink anyway. His mind was in a state of confusion, aggravated by alcohol. He was alone. He was empty. "What have I done? What am I going to do now?" He couldn't just sit there alone indulging in self-pity. He was better than that. He grabbed his coat and walked out of the building not sure which direction to take. His feet led him to an unremarkable night club a few blocks away.

As he walked in he noticed a pair of long legs and a short skirt. Greg walked straight ahead to the bar which brought him right next to the legs. The legs were attached to an hourglass figure with a voice.

"Hi, it said."

He looked at the face and prepared to play the game.

"Hi. You live at the condo's, don't you? Building B, right?" Greg ordered a drink.

"C"

"Right. I've seen you out walking."

"I walk my dog every day."

Cute dog, what's his name?"

The woman sized him up and said, "I don't really have a dog and you never saw me before in your life. But I've seen you. With a woman. You're wife?"

"No, and she found someone else."

"Why?"

"Because fate knew I was going to run into you."

"Oh, brother."

"What, don't you believe in fate?"

"Yes, I do. You know, I can read people pretty well. It's one of my things. Do you want to know what I see?"

"Sure, go ahead. Take your best shot." The conversation had taken a decided turn for the worse but it was better than being alone and you never knew how these things would turn out.

"Oh, I'm not shooting. I'm not the type. But what I see in you is a person who is disconnected from his being. I think as humans we all are to a certain extent. But you seem disconnected on many levels. And I think it hurts you. Did anyone ever tell you that before?"

"No, do you charge for this kind of advice or is it free?"

"This isn't advice. I don't give advice, except one thing.

Don't try to pick me up. I'm not they type."

"What makes you think you're not my type? Maybe I just want some company."

Well that would be great. The truth is that I'm married. My husband is out of town and I just couldn't face being at home alone. I came here to find someone to talk to. I like your attitude, upbeat even though you're down. What's the matter, problems at home?"

"Did I say I was married? Doesn't your husband mind you going to bars alone and talking to strange men?"

"You're not strange and if my husband were here I think he'd agree. If you were strange you wouldn't be sitting there. See that bartender? That's my husband's cousin. So I'm not really alone. And you didn't need to tell me you're married. It's written all over you. I read people, remember. You seem to need someone to talk to.

"Who are you?" Greg asked.

The woman had a nice smile and laugh lines at the corner of her eyes.

"Star. Star Song. My parents were hippies. I always feel the need to explain my name."

"It's a very pretty name. I'm Greg. Jones."

"Well, Greg Jones, if you're not determined to pick someone up tonight we might have an interesting conversation."

"We might at that."

"Hey Charlie, can we have a couple more drinks when you get the chance. I'll have another coke. What are you drinking, Greg Jones? I'll buy."

"Greg, please. I'll have a coke, too."

They talked for hours under the watchful gaze of Cousin Charlie. She asked about his wife and he found himself sharing his story with this strange woman. She didn't judge him at all. Nothing he said seemed unexpected to her. She gave him a fresh perspective, a wife's point of view. And Greg listened to her. She really did seem extraordinarily perceptive.

Greg glanced at his watch and realized how long they had

been sitting and talking. He also realized that he wasn't drunk anymore or as confused as he was when he'd walked into the bar.

"Star, I can't thank you enough. I feel so much better than when I came in. If I didn't know better I would think you're an angel assigned to keep an idiot from spoiling his Thanksgiving with a hangover or worse."

"She's an angel, alright. Everybody thinks so. My cousin's a lucky guy." Charlie made his presence known from time to time.

Star and Greg smiled at each other. "I'm going home and get some sleep. It was very nice to meet you. Happy Thanksgiving."

"Happy Thanksgiving, Greg Jones. I have the feeling that everything will work out just fine for you and your family. Goodbye."

Greg walked back to the condo. Star is a lot like my little sister, Greg thought, as he drifted into the first restful slumber he'd had in many nights.

CHAPTER 10

Responsibility

T he Jones kids woke up excited. It was Thanksgiving and Dad was coming home for dinner. Janet was closest to the door when Greg walked in.

"Daddy!" She ran to him and gave him a hug.

"Hi, honey. I hope I'm not too early."

"I'm glad you came early. I miss you."

"Where is everyone?"

"Mom and Helen are in the kitchen. Cindy went up to her room. And Jason is out by the pool talking on his phone."

Greg could see his son when he looked out the window. Jason was a lonely figure sitting at the table on the patio. His shoulders slumped, his eyes were closed, his forehead rested in his hand.

"Why don't I know what's going on with my own son?" he asked himself.

Jason had always taken his world for granted. He was the first child, having his parent's devotion for almost four years before Janet was born. He had always attracted a lot of attention for his good looks. He got A's in school and was the town football hero. His peers looked up to him like a teen idol. Now, in a matter of months his world had changed. The whole situation was so overwhelming. Jason relied on his newfound relationship with Christ. He had started spending more time at Marcia's house where they lived a Christian lifestyle.

Her parents may have been upset and embarrassed but at least they thought of the baby as a person and not a "pregnancy."

Marcia had passed the first trimester and she was glowing. A sonogram had revealed the baby was a girl. She didn't want to tell anyone. She thought it would be easier to keep referring to her as "the baby" until she knew whether or not it would be a part of her life.

Jason's emotions were tumultuous but he was pretty sure he was in love with Marcia. She was different from the other girls he had dated. She had a strong faith in God and values which were in line with Biblical principles. She had never really been interested in a career. Her parents had insisted she pick something so she had decided on child psychology but she dreaded the thought of more school. And she was scared, now, with an uncertain future hanging over her head.

Jason and Marcia both respected their parents and obeyed the rules, for the most part. Both of their parents wanted to make sure they weren't sleeping together and while Jason couldn't see the harm at this point, he wasn't surprised. So Marcia and he spent as much time together as they could in each other's house, mostly hers. They usually met after school, by the big tree out front. They would walk to Marcia's house where her brothers and sisters and their friends would be having snacks and talking. It was loud and friendly compared to the silence and tension at his house.

In the short time he had known them, he felt more a part of their family then his own. His parents were embroiled in their work and their own problems and apparently didn't have much time or concern for his. At least that's the way it seemed to him most of the time.

Marcia's parents insisted she quit St. Joseph's High after the first half of the year. She would finish her senior year in virtual school. It was one thing to have rumors flowing behind their back but something entirely different for the kids to flaunt their indiscretion in front of the whole community, they said.

Their families were going to try to tell them what to do but Jason and Marcia began making their own plans, preparing for the "meeting" after Thanksgiving.

The first decision they made was to bring this baby into the world. Marcia's family was shocked that they would even consider an abortion. Jason's parents were shocked that they would consider bringing a baby into these circumstances.

The second decision was to find a way to give the baby two parents. If abortion was out then the next logical solution would be adoption. It was a big step for two teenagers. They would have to stop thinking of themselves and start making decisions based on what was best for the baby.

They planned to spend the holiday together. They would spend the morning at the Jones who ate at 12:00. The afternoon they would spend helping at the shelter with the Griffins., serving dinner to the homeless. Afterwards, they would go to Marcia's for another meal and watch the football game on TV.

On the day before Thanksgiving Jason had come to a decision.

Jason woke at 9:30 on Thanksgiving morning and couldn't wait to see Marcia so he called her on her cell.

"Good morning"

She could hear the smile in his voice. "Good morning," she said. "What are you so happy about?"

"I'm looking forward to spending the day together. I wish you could come over right now," he said.

Marcia laughed, "I can make your wish come true. I'm almost ready. I can be there in half an hour."

"Great! We'll have a couple of hours before we eat. I have something I want to ask you. I'll see ya soon."

"What is it? It's no fair making me wait a half an hour."

"I'd rather ask you in person."

"Fine, be that way," she teased. "I'll see you in 20 minutes, then."

"Good. Marcia, I love you," the works came out unbidden.

"What?"

"Never mind. I'll talk to you when you get here, ok?"

"Okay, See ya soon."

After they hung up the phone Jason thought, "I almost blew it. Thank God she didn't hear me. I don't want to blurt it out on the phone like that. I want to do this right, for a change."

Marcia hung up the phone and sat on the edge of her bed in total astonishment. He said, "I love you" I'm sure of it, she thought. He wants to tell me he loves me.

It took her a few minutes to compost herself and then all she wanted was to be with Jason. She rushed out of the house and straight over to the Jones. Jason met her at the door.

"Marcia, do you mind if we go for a walk in the park? I'd like to talk to you alone."

"Sure." Marcia's heart was racing, her stomach doing flip flops.

They walked hand in hand down the block and to the park. Jason stopped at a bench and they sat down.

"Do you remember this place?"

"Oh, Jason. This is where you told me you accepted Christ and that you'd stand by me and our baby."

"I have something else very important to tell you. I love you, Marcia. It's more than having a baby or being in this situation together. I like who you are. I respect you more than any girl I ever met. You're smart. You're fun to be with. You love God as much as I do. I don't know how things are going to turn out, Marcia. But I think we owe it to our baby and ourselves to be a family. It may be hard in the beginning. I don't know how much our parents will be willing to help. But we should at least try, right?" Jason had started to ramble.. Judging by Marcia's shocked look, she didn't agree with him.

"Say something." Jason felt like an idiot. He fought the urge to run. He watched Marcia's expression soften. A single tear moved slowly down her cheek.

"I...I think I must be dreaming. What exactly are you saying, Jason?"

Jason sent a quick prayer, Lord help me, he prayed. He stood and turned to face Marcia. Then to her astonishment he knelt on one knee. "What I'm trying to say is that I love you. Will you marry me?"

"Jason, are you sure? Have you thought this through? You don't have to do this."

"I'm not asking you to marry me because I have to. I love you. I'm sure of it. And I love this baby. I don't want to give it away. I can't stand the thought of having a baby somewhere in the world and not knowing anything about it. Maybe these aren't the best circumstances. But I can't imagine my life without you and our baby in it. Remember in humanities class when we learned about marriage and having a family? They said in the end marriage isn't about love. It's about commitment. I'm telling you that I do love you and I want to make that commitment. And I'm asking you if you feel the same way."

"You know, Jason, I've had a crush on you since the sixth grade. I guess that's not a good reason to have sex but I did. After that when I told you I was pregnant I think I really hated you."

Jason tried to respond.

"No, let me finish. When you told me you accepted Christ I felt so connected to you in a different way. And these last few months, I just don't know what I would have done without you. I love our baby. I want what's best for her. I hadn't even considered getting married knowing how your parents feel. I'm just... I'm really confused."

"Tell me, honestly, how do you feel about me now?"

"I'm pretty sure I love you, too. I think about you all the time. I can feel such a connection through Christ. You're my best friend right now, but then look what we're going through together."

"Don't you think we could stay best friends and go through this life together?"

"Don't you think you're oversimplifying things a little bit?"

"No, I think problems come from overcomplicating things."

"Yeah, well, life is complicated. That's reality. We can't get married because you're dreaming of this perfect simple life where were going to be a perfect family and everything will work out perfectly. Look at your family, Jason, look at what your dad did. Perfection is an illusion."

"Well, I'm not my dad. I can't believe you would compare me with him."

"Sexual indiscretion seems to run in the family."

"You know, I haven't been with anyone else since that night with you. I haven't even seriously considered it. But if that's what you think of me maybe it's time I start going out again."
"Is that what you want to do?"

"NO. No, what I want to do is marry you and find a way to make a home for us, all of us. That's why I brought you here, to the park. I don't want to argue. If you don't want to get married, I guess I understand. I'll just have to get used to the idea, won't I? I'm sorry I brought it up. I didn't mean to put you on the spot. I was trying to be romantic."

"You did good, then. It was definitely romantic."

"We can still be friends, right, at least for the baby's sake?" Jason's eyes began to fill as he thought again of not being a part of his baby's life. "Did you call it her?"

"Yes, it's a girl. I wasn't going to tell anyone; I mean it didn't matter if we were going to give her away."

"A baby girl," said Jason. "I'm going to have a daughter."

"Yes,", said Marcia after a long pause. She leaned in close to him. "I mean, yes to the first part."

"What first part?"

"The part about getting married."

"What? Really?" They reached for each other. "What made you change your mind?"

"You respect me enough to let me go if that's what I want and you love me enough to want to stay friends even if we aren't together. When I think about it the best scenario is being a family. Everything you said makes perfect sense to me."

"Perfect sense, huh?"

They both laughed. "When do you want to tell our families?" Marcia asked.

"Why wait? We're going to see everyone at some point today. Let's announce it at the dinners. That way we can get it over with in one day."

"My parents will have to sign for me. I won't be 18 until May and that's when the baby's due."

"I don't think your parents are going to be the problem."

CHAPTER 11

Thanksgiving

The Jones house smelled scrumptious when Jason and Marcia walked in. Greg weas sitting in the living room with Janet and Cindy. He seemed out of place in his own home. Cindy looked withdrawn as usual. Janet was talking about youth group.

Greg looked up as the young couple came in.

"Hi kids." Greg had noticed the way they looked at each other. I remember when Faith and I looked at each other that way. He knew then that his son had fallen in love. How ironic that they should find love just when his mother and I have lost it, he thought.

"Hi dad," said Jason. The moment was awkward and strained.

"Hi, Mr. Jones," said Marcia.

Jason walked over and sat down. "It's really nice out today. Maybe we can throw the ball around after dinner."

"Sure, son, that would be nice."

"Jason," Marcia interrupted, "Excuse me. I'm going to see if I can help Helen and your mom in the kitchen."

Faith and Helen were busy cutting vegetables. Marcia hadn't eaten breakfast and the aromas were making her stomach growl. She wasn't quite at ease in the unfamiliar kitchen. She was nervous about the announcement she and Jason were planning to make at dinner. She took a deep breath and said a quick prayer. If Faith was going to be her mother-in-law Marcia was determined to make a good impression.

"Is there anything I can do to help?" she said.

"No, we have everything under control, thanks," said Faith.

"You know, I've been making Thanksgiving dinner by myself for as long as I can remember," said Helen, "first for my family when my kids were young and now here. It's nice to have someone in the kitchen to talk to. This is so pleasant. Why don't you have a seat, Marcia, help yourself to a glass of cider."

Marcia looked gratefully at Helen. "Thanks."

"Where are your kids today," Marcia asked Helen.

"They're in their own homes with their own families. We can't all fit in one place anymore so they have their own dinners. When we get done here I'll go visit each of them. When I show up I'm the guest of honor. It suits all of us and cuts way down on the chaos."

"I can understand that. Our family had a reunion one year on Thanksgiving. It took months to arrange. The was no way to make it work for everyone's schedule. We rented the large pavilion at the park so the kids would have plenty of space to play in. It was fun but it was definitely chaotic."

"So, are you going to spend some time with them today?" asked Helen.

Yes, didn't Jason tell you? We always help out at the shelter and then have dinner at home, then watch the game."

Faith had been listening to the exchange. "He hasn't been very forthcoming about his plans lately. I know he's been spending a lot of time at your house."

"Yes," said Marcia. "We've been studying together. I guess we won't be able to after Christmas. My parents want me to finish my senior year in virtual school."

"That will probably be easier for you, especially when you're further along," said Faith.

"That's what mom said." Marica was thinking about missing out on the prom and graduation but she wasn't comfortable enough to say it to Jason's mother.

"Have you chosen an adoption agency?"

Marcia had no idea how to answer Faith's question. She was beginning to be sorry she had come into the kitchen.

She looks like a cornered animal, thought Helen.

"I'm sorry Jason hasn't talked to you, Mrs. Jones," she said. "Maybe I should go and get him?"

"No, Marcia, why don't you just tell me what the two of you have been thinking about?"

"We want to do what's best for the baby."

"That's very commendable. Just what might that be?"

Jason walked into the kitchen as if on cue. He saw his mother first. She was definitely on the offensive and Marcia on defense. "What are you guys talking about?"

"Marcia was just going to enlighten us about what you two have decided would be the best thing for this baby."

"I'm sorry if I haven't talked to you about this, mom. Truth is you've seemed a little distracted. You have a lot on your own plate right now and I wanted to think things through before I said anything. We made a decision this morning and we were going to tell everyone at dinner."

"What do you mean YOU made a decision? I think your parents, Marcia, and Greg and I should be included in any decisions that are made. Exactly what is it you plan to do?"

"Mom, I need you to understand. This is my life, our life. I wanted to make an announcement at dinner. Can't you just wait a little and let us do this our way?"

Faith thought it was one of the most mature things she had ever heard Jason say. "Who are you and what have you done with my son, "she smiled. Jason sounded so sure of himself.

"I guess I have to respect your wishes. I'll be in my room dressing for dinner."

After Faith left the room Helen said, "Did you give any thought as to how your news might affect everyone's digestion?"

They all laughed. It felt good to defuse the awkward situation and vent a little emotion.

"Oh, Lord, what have we gotten ourselves into," Jason prayed.

"It will be okay. You have to make a choice: do what your parents want you to do or what you think is best. If you decide to make decisions for yourself, you have to be prepared to take responsibility for yourself and face the consequences. If you've thought it through and want to make your own choices then you will have to make a stand, sooner or later. I'm proud of you both, regardless of what you decide. You made a mistake but you're facing it together. It shows maturity. Life is full of mistakes and consequences. This won't be the last one, it's part of being an adult. Your lives have changed and can never be the same. And that's also part of life."

Helen's words of wisdom and support helped Jason and Marcia find courage to face the coming confrontation. The three of them worked to mash the potatoes and make gravy. Janet and Greg came in, eagerly looking at the food. "That smells so good, can we help?"
"Your timing is excellent," said Helen. "If you fill the water glasses and help put the food on the table we can eat."

"I'm all for that," said Greg.

"Will you send Cindy to tell Faith that we will be ready to sit down to dinner in a few minutes." Asked Helen.

After everyone was settled at the dining room table, Faith asked Helen to say Grace.

"I'd be happy to, do you mind if we take a moment to say what we're grateful for? It's a tradition in my family."

After a moment Helen started. "I'm grateful for this family, for the chance to be a blessing and also be blessed by you."

Jason said, "I'm grateful for my family." He was thinking of his parents and sisters but also of the new family he would be starting soon.

Marcia said, "I thank God for this wonderful meal and the chance to be here with all of you"

Greg was also grateful for his family and that they were all together that day.

"I'm grateful for my own salvation and Jesus who died for our sins." Janet was still in awe of the difference Christ had made in her life.

Next was Faith's turn. She was at a loss to think of anything to be grateful for with her family in such turmoil. "I'm grateful for my children," she made sure to leave Greg out. "I'm glad we're together this Thanksgiving."

Cindy was sitting with her chin on her chest. "Honey, do you want to say something you're thankful for?" said Faith.

"Everything everyone else said, "Cindy responded.

"May we say Grace?" said Helen.

"Lord we thank you for this wonderful meal. Please bless it that we may do your will. Thank you for this family, Lord. Be with us all in times of need. Guide us in your spirit that any decisions will be in line with your work. We know that change is inevitable. Be with us all in the days ahead and help us all be truly thankful. Amen."

Everyone started quietly serving themselves. Dinner seemed even more special this year because they all helped make it. Conversation picked up while they passed the delicious dishes and slowed again when they all started eating.

After a few minutes of eating Faith looked at Jason and said, "Okay, what's up?"

Jason looked at Marcia, took a deep breath and said, "I asked Marcia to marry me this morning and she said yes."

Everyone froze, staring at him.

Faith was the first to speak. She'd been hoping he wasn't going to say what she'd just heard. "Jason, you said you both wanted what was best for the baby. Do you really think this is best?"

"I do. I love Marcia, mom. She's strong and sweet. She's the kind of girl you settle down with. The timing isn't great but that doesn't mean we can't have a great life together. I don't want some other man being a father to my daughter."

"Your daughter?" Faith was at a loss for words.

"It's a girl?" asked Janet. "You're getting married and having a baby girl? Oh, my gosh, Jason. Congratulations! When are you getting married? Oh, Marcia, we have a lot to do. There's the wedding shower, the baby shower and getting a dress…"

Faith interrupted, "Janet, stop! What are you thinking, Jason? What about college?"

"I have my football scholarship. I'm going to go. I'll get my associates to start and work on the rest a little at a time. I can take some classes online. I'll get there, it'll just take longer."

"Jason, you don't know what you're saying. You're setting yourself up on a very hard road."

"I know that mom. But I can't deal with the idea that someone else will bring up my little girl. People do this kind of thing all the time and have great lives. My priorities have changed. Money isn't the most important thing, right?"

"Says the boy who always had everything handed to him. What do your parents think about this, Marcia?" asked Faith.

"We haven't told my parents yet."

Greg spoke up, then. "Jason, I'm proud of you for wanting to face your responsibilities. I'm not saying I agree with your decision, but you're almost eighteen and about to be a father. If you're ready to start thinking about what's best for those you love then I will support your decision"

"How can you say that? This isn't what's best for them," said Faith.

"Mom, it's my decision. It's what I want. I don't think I could handle not being with Marcia and my daughter. I won't turn my back on them. I wish you would be happy for us. Either way, we're getting married, I'm going to be a father and you are going to be grandparents."

Faith closed her eyes and rubbed her forehead. How had they all come to this? She knew Jason was making the choice for a life that was completely different than the one she wanted for him. He'd had so much potential. But if Jason was determined to marry Marcia and start a family, there wasn't much she could do to stop him. She was going to be a grandmother, that much was true. Did she want her grandchild, granddaughter, adopted by another family to raise? Not to have her here for holidays and family gatherings? She hadn't thought of these things before and her mind was a whirlwind.

Faith opened her eyes and looked around the table. Janet and Helen were staring at their plates. Cindy was looking around at each person sitting at the table. Jason and Marcia were holding hands and looking at each other. Greg was looking at her and the mixed emotions when their eyes met was overwhelming. But she knew one thing for sure. Her family was drifting apart and she couldn't let that happen. If she didn't support Jason she could lose him. Maybe that's what Greg was thinking.

"Well, I guess we'd better plan a wedding," she said. "Thanks, mom, you're the best," said Jason.

When Marcia and Jason arrived at Marcia's house they decided not to wait to tell their news.

"Could we talk before we go to the shelter?"

"Of course."

"Mom, dad, I'm getting married."

In the stunned silence, both Jason and Marcia imagined they would go through the same scene they had just come up against at the Jones house. Prepared for the worst, they were surprised when Meg Griffin said, "Thank God, I was hoping to be a part of this baby's life."

"It's a girl, mom."

"I don't know what your plans are but you can count on us doing all we can to help. You don't know what you're in for doing this. But I'll trust in the Lord to see you through. I think taking responsibility is the right thing to do."

They all hugged, united in determination and an uncertain future.

The rest of the day was spent in love and Thanksgiving. Jason thought about the difference between Marcia's family and his own. Their priorities were so different. A thought came clearly into his mind, "Trust in me." He knew that trusting in God was a big part of the difference in their families. He would do all he could to remember it in the difficult times that must result from the decision they had made.

CHAPTER 12

Christmas Miracle

December was a cascade of activity. Christmas was always a busy time for the Jones. This year there was the added stress of a divided family. Faith was preparing for her job in France. Janet and Carol decided to throw a baby shower. They would invite everyone who knew about the pregnancy. It would be small but they would be celebrating the baby girl instead of mourning her loss. And there was a wedding to plan.

Faith couldn't remember ever feeling so drained. She knew she was spread too thin. She focused her attention on work, something she could control.

She seldom saw Greg but as Christmas approached thoughts of him came unbidden to interfere with and already overloaded mind. Outwardly Faith seemed calm and collected. But inside was mayhem and confusion. Her life was out of control and she didn't know what to do.

On Christmas morning Faith was exhausted. She was so glad the holidays were almost over and things could get back to normal. She wondered what Greg was doing. She wasn't looking forward to spending the day with him. Lord, help he get through this day, she thought.

Greg woke Christmas morning to silence. No decorations

were in the condo. The kids weren't there to wake him up and the excitement was missing. Faith had asked him to wait until afternoon to come home. The way she had asked, in quiet desperation, he had agreed. He knew that tone in her voice. She was almost at the end of her rope. So much had happened, so many changes. Here he was, feeling sorry for himself for being away from his family while Faith was at home carrying the ball.

He was finally seeing things from her point of view. Her security was gone, her trust betrayed. Greg couldn't stay in the condo anymore. He couldn't bear it, he had to get out. He didn't know where to go. He had already put Faith through enough. It hit him then like the proverbial ton of bricks. He loved her. He loved her so much, and he had hurt her. He had alienated himself from his family. It had happened little by little over the years as his secret took more and more of his time and attention.

He dressed and went out. It was cold and just as quiet outside as it was inside. Bleak, that was the word. It described what he saw and it described how he felt. He had nowhere to go, nothing to do, so he walked. He didn't see one person, only a few cars. Most people were at home, with their families. He thought of his own family and of Faith, his beautiful, loving wife.

He remembered their life together objectively, as from a distance. They had met in college at a football game, with a group of kids. They liked each other right away and before the evening was over Greg had her phone number.

Their romance lasted through college. Greg didn't want to commit and they both wanted financial security, so marriage wasn't something they considered until after college. But they had so much in common and their relationship was comfortable from the start.

Greg knew that Faith was the girl for him. When all their friends started getting married after college he decided it was time. He proposed in the traditional way, on bended knee.

She was so beautiful on their wedding day. He had felt such overwhelming love for her then as he felt right now. How did that feeling get lost in the shuffle?

He remembered Faith after Jason was born. Her face was radiant, their love tangible. His mind went to a moment when he and Faith were kissing in the pool while a young Jason and Janet played nearby. Funny how those small, spontaneous moments of intense emotions can stay so fresh in our memories, he thought.

Faith wasn't happy about her third pregnancy at first but after Cindy was born Faith seemed to accept it. She had found a true inner peace. She was a devoted mother and wife, but when she started working again some things had changed. Helen took care of the house and kids after she was hired, but no one was really taking care of him, anymore. He had never said anything to Faith about his feelings. Part of their plan for their life was that Faith would work outside of the home. Faith needed outside interests and it would allow them to do whatever they wanted when it came time to retire.

That was about the time I got involved with Ann, he thought. What kind of man does that make me? Faith was experiencing the light of Christ and I was repelled by it. Could I have affected my whole family without even knowing it? He saw Janet prancing around in a thong bathing suit, Jason getting that girl pregnant, sweet Cindy all alone, and Faith spending less time at home and more time at work. It ended with him here, all alone on Christmas morning walking without a destination.

"Oh, Dear God, what have I done? How could I be so blind?" Greg had stopped walking. He couldn't go on. He had failed his family, himself and his God. He had believed his own lies and excuses.

"I go to church, Lord, I believe in you. How could you let this happen?" Looking up he asked, "What do I do now?" He realized then that he had stopped in front of a church.

Greg had gone to church every Sunday for most of his life. He was a member; he was a Christian, and he had been baptized. He was one of the righteous, wasn't he? Didn't he deserve special protection? Wasn't he better than the average person?

His eyes focused on a stained-glass window, a picture representing Jesus. Greg had seen that window so many times but today it seemed to have a presence. Jesus appeared to be walking toward Greg, His arms outstretched, a look of profound peace and love on His face. The moment of overwhelming despair tore down the walls between his Savior and himself. "I need you, Lord, please help me."

Greg walked up to the church and opened the door; there had probably been a Sunrise Service not that long ago. The beautifully decorated sanctuary was so comforting compared to the stark emptiness he had experienced so far that morning. He continued to the front of the church completely aware of the Holy Spirit and humbled in a way he had never been before. Greg was standing on a precipice, his sins behind him and the light in front. A leap of faith was imminent but he had no idea how to proceed. He decided to just speak his thoughts.

"What have I done, Lord? What do I do now? This guilt is more than I can bear. I know I don't deserve forgiveness, but I ask you, Lord, if not for me then for my family. Come into my heart, Lord, forgive ne and cleanse me. I know I can't do it alone."

As Greg felt the pure love of God flow into him he was aware that he had changed and could never be the same again." He finally understood that he belonged to God, as a son to a father. Freedom from guilt and shame washed over him and brought him to his knees. Now he knew the meaning of "washed clean by the blood of Christ," for it was the birth of Christ and His death that made it possible for a strong man like Greg Jones to be healed in an instant and the course of his life to be changed forever. He realized he had never really been in control of other people or most circumstances and he gave the reins to Christ. God's profound love made Greg feel full and complete.

Greg sat in the church for a long time, just thinking. He wondered what had taken him so long to understand salvation. The information was there all the time. Why had he resisted? Maybe he would find out some day. Right now he had to find a way to fix the problems he had created. He had no idea that one by one his family was being healed. He only knew his place was with them. He would work to stay in God's will. He knew that meant keeping his family together. Greg hoped that God would show him a way.

Greg walked out of the church with a renewed spirit. His heightened awareness made him realize just how far he had strayed from his family. He knew in their minds nothing had changed but in his heart everything was different. How would he make his family see it? He wanted to go straight home, wanted to show them he had changed. But he knew it would be a mistake to barge in unannounced. He didn't want to start this special day by putting up Faith's defenses. Greg realized he hadn't even showered and shaved.

"I look like hell. How long have I been looking like this?" he asked himself. In truth, he had been looking rather scruffy for weeks. "How could I have let myself go like this?" he thought.

Greg went back to the condo and got a shower. He thought about the gifts he had for his family. He had bought Cindy a set of first addition books, Janet a cashmere sweater, Jason a football jersey worn by his favorite player and Faith an emerald necklace. The gifts were okay but not enough to show the people dearest to him how much they meant. Nothing in the world could convince them. How could he start healing his family? "What should I do, God?"

At 11:00 Greg called home. Janet answered the phone. "Hi, dad. When are you coming?"

With that simple statement his anxiety evaporated. Of course his children still loved him. Of course they wanted him to be there on Christmas morning.

"Is your mom there, honey? I'd like to talk to her."

"Yeah, okay, dad. See ya soon, right?"

"I'll be over as soon as I can."

"Okay," Janet said.

How many times have I let her down? Oh, God, I'm so sorry. And the still small voice said," You have been forgiven."

"Merry Christmas, Greg," said Faith. She sounded deflated. He had hurt her so much. God had forgiven me but my family hasn't, he realized.

"Merry Christmas, Faith. I didn't want to come over without calling. Is now a good time?"

Greg heard a big sigh. "Now's fine," she said.

Christmas carols were playing when he walked in the door. "Where is everyone," he called.

"In here, Dad," the voice came from the kitchen.

"Look what Helen made." On the table was a beautiful tray of fruit and one of blueberry muffins. The kids were sipping mugs of hot chocolate.

"Would you like a cup of coffee?" Helen asked.

"Love it, thanks."

"I'm going, then." Helen spent Christmas visiting her family and friends.

Sitting chatting with the kids and looking around Greg felt like a stranger in his own house. This wasn't the usual Christmas morning. "Who wants to open presents?"

"Mom said to wait for her," Janet said.

"I'm here, let's go!" Faith said, walking into the room.

"Yay!" the Jones kids chorused.

They all piled into the living room. "I think I see some Christmas Spirit," said Greg.

They took turns choosing presents. Cindy was first and chose a present for Faith. It was a candle in a basket with flowers arranged around it. She had made it for her mom at Girl Scouts. Then Faith chose one for Jason.

The stress evaporated and, for this moment, they were a family again. The unspoken pain receded and they relished the feeling of love, alive in the room, for God was there with them. His Spirit was at work in the Jones household.

The atmosphere was warm. They laughed and enjoyed being together, again. Greg realized that the gift that meant most to his kids was his being here, the gift of time.

"So, what are your plans for the day," asked Greg.

Jason and I are planning to go the Christmas service at

church," said Janet.

"Dad, there's something you should know," Jason chimed in. "It's the most amazing thing. Janet and I both accepted Christ. Not at the same time, but close. We're on fire for Him and trying to live our lives as God wants us to."

Greg felt as if time stood still. No words came to his mind. He was elated, astonished, dumbfounded and profoundly grateful.

Janet misunderstood his silence as disapproval.

"Dad, you may not understand this but believe me when I tell you it's made all the difference in the world to our lives."

"No, Janet, it's...I just...I don't know how to say this. I had a similar experience this morning. It seems too good to be true. I never thought that we could all be together on this. I just...I don't know what to say."

"Oh, dear God," Janet said. They ran together and hugged. Faith joined in, careful not to touch Greg. Greg picked up Cindy and they had a moment of unity that each person had doubted would ever come again. It was truly a miracle, a Christmas miracle.

The day was comfortable between Greg and his kids. Even Faith was cordial while maintaining distance. They all prepared the meal together. The prayer was one of thanksgiving and commitment. After dinner Jason, Janet and Greg went to Christmas Service. Cindy said she didn't feel well so Faith stayed home with her.

Later they made a fire and played games while watching White Christmas on TV. To the kids it seemed like everything was back to normal. Even better in some ways since dad was hanging out with them instead of working in his study. It got late and Cindy looked like she was going to fall asleep. "Cindy, honey, why don't you go to bed?" said Faith.

"No, I'm not sleepy," she said. But she wasn't fooling anyone. No one wanted the day to end. It had all been so wonderful.

"Come on, Cindy. Jason and I will take you up," Janet said.

Greg saw a look pass between Janet and Jason. He looked at Faith and knew she'd seen it, too. They obviously wanted to give their parents some time together.

"Night, mom. Night, dad." They called as they went upstairs.

"Night kids," they both said.

A strained silence settled on the room. They avoided looking at each other for some seconds until finally their eyes met.

Greg saw pain on Faith's face. He saw anger there, too. The day had done much to defuse her anger but it was still evident in her eyes.

What Faith saw when she looked at him was regret and resolve. She could see his love for her as if he were speaking to her with his eyes.

All at once Faith felt exhausted. She was tired of the hurt and anger. She was tired of trying to help the kids understand something which made no sense to her. And she was tired from the holidays and its added responsibilities on an already full schedule. He reached out to her and she allowed him to put his arm around her. It felt so good to be held even though in the back of her mind she knew it wasn't this easy to make things right. But just for a moment, at the end of a beautiful day, she enjoyed the memory of how it used to be. Love overpowered the pain. Neither spoke, not wanting to break the spell. Eventually Faith succumbed to exhaustion and sleep took her.

Greg didn't move, he barely breathed. He knew if Faith woke up she'd ask him to leave so she could go to bed. And he would have to go back to the condo alone. He was tired, too. Today had been an emotional rollercoaster ride, from the depths of despair to the pinnacle of peace with Jesus as his guide. He was still in awe that both Janet and Jason had accepted Christ. The day had been so peaceful and perfect. He knew without a doubt that it was the Holy Spirit at work. Greg realized that with Christ in his heart and Faith's head resting on his shoulder he was complete in a way he had never been before. He prayed a prayer of thanksgiving and total submission to his Lord's will.

Faith woke awoke in his arms around 2:00 AM. As Greg suspected, she went up to bed. But she insisted it would be much safer for him to sleep on the couch.

Faith was confused. She had gotten used to the idea that her husband was a jerk and her marriage had ended. She was getting ready to start another chapter in her life that didn't include Greg. Freedom like she hadn't known in so long beckoned her.

As she lay in bed unable to get back to sleep, she thought it had been a special day. He was attentive, thoughtful and, yes, loving. But how long would that last? He never even said he was sorry or tried to explain himself. I wouldn't have believed him, anyway, but he could have at least tried. It's obvious we still love each other. We have our marriage and the kids. What am I going to do?

Hours later she finally slept and when she awoke Greg was gone. She felt an odd mixture of disappointment and relief. Her confusion lingered all day. Christmas had fallen on Friday this year and the Country Club suspended all health club classes for the week.

The kids went to the movies at the mall but she decided not to go. Faith roamed around the house restless and unsure, torn between the longing for love and security and an uncertain future. Her anger towards Greg was relentless but the feelings from Christmas were also there. The wonderful memories of their life together mingled with betrayal. Love and hate at war within her. Which one would win? She felt empty and alone. She got on her exercise bike and put on the news, something to fill her mind and keep her busy. It didn't stop the turmoil in her mind but it was easier to bear. Christmas was lovely but it was over. Time to move forward, start a new chapter in her life.

CHAPTER 13

Separation

New Year's Eve had come and gone. Faith was putting away Christmas decorations, trying to get the house back in order. Her thoughts strayed to the New Year's Eve party at the club. It was strange to be there alone. Greg had decided not to go. She watched as other couples kissed at midnight. It had brought a feeling of profound loss.

Now it was a brand-new year, a fresh start. Faith had always loved the first day of a new year. This year she was going to France. She would be leaving in two days. She thought about Christmas day and Greg. Could it be possible that things would work out? They obviously still loved each other. There just wasn't any way to know for sure before she was scheduled to leave and nothing could convince Faith to give up the chance of a lifetime. No, she thought, things could never be the same. She had been living a lie. Greg had been skirting around behind her back. How could she ever trust him again? One beautiful Christmas day can't take away the hurt and anger.

Just then the phone rang. It was Greg.

"Hi, Faith."

"Hi."

"You're probably packing, getting ready to go. I'd like to talk to you before you leave. Can we get together for coffee or something?"

"I don't think there is anything to say. Nothing can change what you did. I really am busy, Greg."

"I know, Faith. You have no idea how I wish I could change what I did. But I want to talk to you about the kids. With you away I think I should spend more time at the house. I want to make sure that's okay with you."

"I have a problem with you bringing your girl friends over."

"I'm not seeing her anymore. I'm not seeing anyone. I'm trying to make amends. I can't take back the past, Faith. But I have to believe that doing the right thing now counts for something."

"Whatever, Greg. I really am kind of busy. If you want to play the good guy now, I guess I can't stop you."

"I really appreciate this, Faith. And, honey, if there's anything I can do for you once you're in France I hope you'll let me know. I'll do anything I can."

"Greg, I don't know what to say to you other than too little, too late. And don't "honey" me. I'm glad you'll be there for the kids. I think they will appreciate it. Just leave me out of it. Okay?"

Faith was confident that Jason and Janet would be fine. They would miss her, of course, as she would miss them. Jason had some growing up to do and decisions to make. He seemed to be on the right path. And Helen would be here. Faith respected Helen and knew she could be trusted to give the right kind of advice. But Faith wasn't as sure about Cindy. The young girl had become more and more isolated. She had responded at Christmas, though, when her dad was here. This must be so hard on her, Faith thought. Maybe Greg would step up to the plate and spend some time with her, especially after I leave."

Time flew by for Faith in a flurry of plans and packing. She had misgivings at times but Helen had moved in and the household was smooth and efficient. The kids were back into their daily routine.

When the day came for her to leave, the kids were despondent.

"I'll be back in a couple of weeks. Your job is to do your

schoolwork and listen to Helen. You can call me any time you want. It'll be okay, you'll see." Faith said with more confidence than she felt.

"I just don't know how you can leave us at a time like this. Have you prayed about this, mom? Are you sure you know what you're doing?" asked Janet.

"Janet, in my entire adult life I've never found a time that was convenient for pursuing my own career. I don't think there ever will be. But the opportunity is now. And I think everything is going to be just fine. Helen's here full time and your dad is planning to be here more. You won't even notice I'm gone with school and everything. And I'll be back in a few weeks."

"What about Cindy? I think she's in real trouble, mom."

"Cindy's going to be just fine. She's in a funk right now, but she a very sensitive girl. She just needs to see that everything is going to work out. Do what you can to encourage and motivate her, okay?"

Okay, mom, I'll do my best."

"I know I can count on you, Janet. Thanks."

Her family was changing. She could see the differences in Janet and Jason. Jason had accepted fatherhood. He and Marcia were spending a lot of time together. They were involved in church activities and spent lots of time at each other's house. Janet was also involved the youth group. She seemed to have a new group of friends almost overnight. She looked younger, these days. She wore less make-up and more clothing. She didn't look like she was trying so hard to attract boys. Janet was always tasteful and pretty but now she looked beautiful and glowing.

Jason put his mom's bags in the trunk. Marcia got in the back seat and Jason went to get Cindy. He found her lying on her bed crying.

"Come on Cindy, do you want mom to go away seeing you cry like this? It's bad luck. Let's take her to the airport and try to send her off smiling."

"She doesn't care about me, why should I care about her?"

Jason didn't know what to do except leave her alone. He

assumed his mom knew what she was doing and that Cindy would be fine.

"Mom, Cindy really doesn't want to go to the airport. Can't she just stay here with Helen? No point forcing her to go. She'll just pout and cry the whole time."

"You're probably right. She'll be fine when she sees how well this is going to work out."

Jason, Janet, and Marcia watched the plane take off through the fence outside the terminal. They watched it fly out of sight knowing their life was about to change. They wondered if Faith would ever come home. Sometimes, they knew, parents left and didn't come back.

Faith boarded the plane with mixed feelings. The look on her children's faces haunted her. She wondered, again, whether she was doing the right thing. She told herself the decision had already been made. Of course there would be hardships, as with anything, she reasoned away the doubts. She started thinking about her new project. It was going to be the highlight of her career up to now. She couldn't wait to get started. In truth she was thankful to be getting away from the situations at home over which she had no control.

It was early Friday afternoon; she would arrive in France on Saturday morning. She would have to rent a car and drive more than an hour to a small town where she would be staying at a Bed and Breakfast close to the property. That way she could get settled and look over the property at her leisure during the weekend. She had looked at pictures, of course, and read the descriptions. It looked like a fascinating place.

The description said, "large farmhouse, built in the 1700's, needs renovation." She thought that might be an understatement judging by the picture. But the house and property were huge, more than 80 hectares, or over 200 acres. There were two barns, a stable and a carriage house. There was an attic and even a cave to explore. Faith could barely contain her excitement.

Saturday morning Faith settled into her room. She was impatient and restless and decided to drive out to the project instead of waiting.

Everything was in a state of disrepair. They planned to gut the existing structures and renovate instead of tearing them down. That was part of the sales agreement and she was passionate about keeping the historical ambiance.

She checked out the farmhouse. First. Faith was a little worried that the floor wasn't safe, but her curiosity overcame her fear as she made her way through the huge old house. This was more like a manor with servant quarters and a kitchen that boasted a walk-in fireplace and very large wood burning stove which was probably state of the art in its day. Upstairs there were many bedrooms, some with adjoining sitting areas. There was a wing that had obviously been a nursery. There was still some old furniture and a couple of old, tattered trunks in the attic. She could have spent a week there, looking into every corner and imagining a busy household and planning the new designs. She could envision a pool in the courtyard, done in a Tahitian style. They could incorporate the unique styles from the French Islands in each building.

Faith didn't explore the barns and carriage house as thoroughly as the house. She thought it would be best to make sure they were safe, first. The cave was a depression that went deep into the rock. Faith thought it would be the perfect place for a salt cave, a place to relax and detox.

She spent the next weeks working with the architect and designer, who were making rough designs for each building. She would be the middleman, eyes and ears for the Board of Directors. The goal was to create a luxury health spa where anyone could come and rejuvenate. From the décor to the menu, it would all be centered on health. The Country Club in the states was much more community centered so this was a new direction for them.

After the construction was done it would be Faith's project to hire the staff, some from the club back in the states, and set up the management of new luxury accommodations for people who wanted to "get away from it all." During the renovation there wouldn't be much for her to do other than oversee. But coming in on the very beginning and helping to design the whole estate was beyond thrilling for her and she was honored to be the one chosen.

Three weeks flew by. Faith wasn't looking forward to going home except to see her kids. Home was full of pain and sadness. It brought her down. But she wouldn't disappoint her kids, so she boarded the plane and made the long trip back to the states.

The house was quiet when Faith walked in. She could tell that Greg had been spending time there. His umbrella was in the foyer, his favorite coffee in the kitchen. The pillows in the den were piled into the corner of the couch the way he liked them. When she sat down she could smell his cologne. She walked through the house filled with mixed emotions. It felt good to be back and she was exhausted. But the reminders of Greg's betrayal were like a punch in her stomach, the quiet house a reminder of emptiness and loss.

Faith's weekend drew slowly towards its conclusion. She looked forward to going back to France.

Helen had gone to check on her apartment and stayed there while Faith was home. Jason and Janet were busy with youth group. Cindy was in her room, laying on the bed, somewhere between awake and asleep. Faith came and sat beside her, pulled her close and kissed her forehead.

"I guess it's just you and me," said Faith.

"I don't feel very good, mom," said Cindy.

"What's wrong, honey, are you sick?" asked Faith.

"No, I'm just kind of tired. I just want to lay here for a little while."

"Tell you what, why don't we go downstairs? We can watch some TV together. Wouldn't that be nice?"

"I guess so," Cindy said.

After Faith boarded the plane for France, the stress she didn't even realize was there seemed to seep from her being. Her room at the B&B beaconed her like home.

She loved the feeling of freedom she got from being in France. It was like living another life. In France she was in control and respected. The architect was doing an amazing job on the plans for the club. It was more than she had hoped. The people that got involved were like-minded and worked well together. She felt calm and self-assured.

At home it was completely the opposite. She felt like she didn't have any control at all. Her friends and some of the people at the club and at church looked at her with pity. Others seemed disgusted at the scandal.

Although Faith missed fer family terribly at times, she found herself preferring to be in France. Traveling home was difficult and exhausting. Several times she skipped the scheduled trip home telling the kids that she was just too tired, which was true.

Thousands of miles away in The States, the Jones kids wondered if they were losing their mom and their dad.

CHAPTER 14

Getting Help

Cindy sat on the porch swing listening to it creak as it went slowly back and forth. She was tired and her head hurt. No one bothered her here except the neighbors, to say hi when they went past. She was invisible to her family and she liked it that way. If no one noticed her they wouldn't being tell her to leave them alone.

She knew something was wrong with her. Janet and her mom were mad at her because she was tired. No one else she knew was sad all the time like she was. She was letting her coach down. She wasn't getting any badges done for girl scouts. Her teachers were disappointed in her grades which were slipping. It all made her so tired. She just wanted to go to sleep and shut out everything. Cindy went through the motions of her day. She did what she was told as if automated and looking through a fog.

When someone asked her what was wrong she said, "Nothing." But how can an eight-year-old little girl express feelings that she hasn't the words for? How could she tell them that she knew she was worthless? They already knew it or they wouldn't be looking at her that way.

Something had snapped inside of Cindy. If all her hard work and second place wasn't good enough then nothing she ever did would be. She just wasn't good enough. She gave up. She stopped participating in school, scouts, and gymnastics. She wanted to quit but they wouldn't let her. She wanted to lay in bed and sleep but someone was always waking her up and telling her to do something. At least here, on the porch swing they left her alone.

Daddy had moved out first, then mom. She said it was for work but it was the same thing as moving out, she was gone. Half of her family was missing. In her mind she knew that she was a disappointment and whatever was wrong was her fault.

The bright spot in her life was Helen. She was Cindy's lifeline. It was Helen who was waiting with a snack when she got home, Helen who picked her up from practice, Helen who helped with projects and homework. Helen made her supper and tucked her into bed. Janet was busy at the church and with her new friends. Jason was at Marcia's a lot after practice. Daddy only came on weekends but she saw him more now than she used to and he made her feel a little better when he came over. He stayed sometimes until bedtime and tucked Cindy in.

Cindy woke one morning feeling sick in the stomach and with a headache. She looked pale; her eyes were puffy. Helen thought she looked kind of thin. "Why didn't I notice this before?" she thought. Helen kept Cindy home from school and made an appointment with the doctor for that afternoon. Cindy went back to bed and fell asleep instantly.

Later at the doctor's office, the nurse weighed her and as suspected, she had lost 5 pounds. The doctor examined Cindy and then asked her to wait in the children's area while he talked to Helen.

"I don't want to alarm you and her parents, he said, but 5 pounds is a significant loss for someone her age and size. I don't think we should take it lightly. I want to do some tests. We'll start with blood work and see if we can't figure out what's going on with her. Has she been sick a lot lately?"

"She's been down in the dumps lately and things are hard at home right now, but this is the first time since, probably last spring that she's complained about being sick. What do you think it is?"

"Her vitals are good and there's no fever. The next step is to do some tests. We can take blood samples right here in the office and let you know the results in a couple of days."

Helen took a deep breath and told herself there was no use getting upset until she knew if something was wrong. She hoped it was just a cold or something. She thought about calling Faith but decided she'd wait until she had something to tell her. No use upsetting her and making her worry with no reason. Helen would worry enough for both.

Greg came over that night to talk to Helen about what the doctor said.

"You know, for some time now I've been noticing a change in her. She looks so serious all the time. She used to laugh and giggle but now... I think things have been hard on her." said Helen.

I haven't called Faith, yet. I was going to wait until the test results. There's no use both of us worrying and nothing we can do about it tonight. Especially if it's nothing serious.

Greg knew that Faith would want to be informed but he agreed that there wouldn't be anything she could do and it was a little premature to worry Faith when Cindy could be sick with a cold.

Greg stayed for dinner with the kids, all the while watching Cindy. She looked sad, didn't say anything, and didn't eat much. Greg realized that he didn't know how long she'd been that way. Until recently he hadn't spent much time there with his kids. But when he was honest with himself, he realized that he'd never really gotten to know his youngest child.

Several days later the Doctor called the Jones house.

"The blood tests came back normal," Doctor G said, "I've known Cindy since the day she was born and yesterday she seemed unusually quiet. You mentioned that things are hard at home, Helen, is it something that would upset an eight-year-old?"

"It's actually more than one thing," answered Helen. "And yes, I think she is upset. You should probably talk to her parents about it. Mrs. Jones is out of town but I can ask Mr. Jones to call you."

Greg called the doctor a few hours later.

"Hey, doc, what's going on with my little girl?"

"Well, Greg, the tests didn't turn up anything. Helen says there may be some stress at home. I'm going to recommend a psychological evaluation."

"Oh, you're kidding. There is some stress right now, doc. But that's not unusual in life. We'll work through it. What doesn't kill you makes you stronger, right?"

"UM, well, Helen thinks she's been moody longer than a couple of months and I remember thinking she looked depressed shortly after summer vacation. It could be nothing, Greg. I'm just saying we should explore all possibilities."

"Yes, of course,. What's our next step?"

"I'll order this evaluation and see if that turns up anything."

"You know best, George."

It was two weeks until the evaluation. Cindy complained often that her stomach hurt and her head ached.

Faith came home a week early so she could go to the doctor with Cindy. She arrived on Friday for one full week at home. Faith knew that her decision to go to France had added to Cindy's condition and she felt guilty for that. But she was sure that the main reason Cindy was upset was because of Greg's absence. He was the guilty one. She hadn't done anything wrong.

The next morning, over coffee, Faith talked to Helen about it.

"I'm just not sure what you can do to help her at this point," said Helen. "I guess they have to figure out what's wrong first and then what to do about it. Maybe they'll have a better idea by the next time you come home."

"Do you think my working in France could have made Cindy sick?" asked Faith.

"I think there's a lot more to it," Helen was trying not to take sides. But the truth was that she was on the side of the children. "Greg is going to take Cindy to her appointment. He wants to be the one to explain, you know, what's going on at home."

"I wonder what his version will sound like. That's why I came home, I plan to take her."

"The doctor might think it will benefit Cindy to have both of you there," Helen said.

Cindy's evaluation was a series of tests including ordering more blood tests and an MRI. Faith and Greg took her to her first appointment together. A few weeks later when Faith came back to the states, she and Greg went together to discuss the diagnosis.

"Your daughter is in a deep depression," he said. "She has a chemical imbalance which has probably been there for some time. I would like to prescribe an anti-depressant for her and see her every week to start. She will need to be monitored closely at first for side effects."

"What can we expect, doctor?"

"The good news is that I don't see any signs of other serious disorders. But I caution you to take this very seriously. Disorders are hard to diagnose in children. Left untreated, this condition could potentially become much worse. These cases can often be treated and the balance restored. Either way, there isn't any reason she can't resume a normal life once we find the right medication. You should see an improvement with her ability to deal with her daily life within three weeks. If not, we'll try another medication. We will work on positive coping skills in therapy. Again, she will need to be monitored closely and helped to learn to use these skills. It's hard to say what the long-term outcome will be. I've been working with kids for fifteen years. Cindy is a kind and sensitive girl. I think she has the benefit of a stable, loving family. I understand you're going through some tough times right now, that may be what brought on the behavior changes. But the imbalance was already there. It's important for her to know that you are both there for her. Be kind and understanding. Let her know that the problems you are having aren't her fault. In these cases children often blame themselves for family problems. Don't push her too hard for the present. Let's see how the medication works and go from there."

"I'm not sure what I can do about getting home more often," said Faith.

"Well, Mrs. Jones, while being home with Cindy would be the best-case scenario, for now we are working on her chemical imbalance. I'd like you to bring her to her appointment when you are home. Mr. Jones can bring her when you're not. Your involvement is paramount. Your nightly phone call will be important, too. She may not talk much but it could be devastating to her if you missed a call."

"I understand, doctor. I'll leave you my contact information. Please call me for anything, day or night," said Faith.

"That goes for me, too, doctor. Thank you for everything," said Greg.

CHAPTER 15

Holy Spirit

"Sometimes we just have to wonder what good could possibly come out of our present circumstance. In Romans 8:28 God promises that all things work together for good to those who love Him, to those who are called according to His purpose. We accept that. But when disaster follows disaster and yet more disaster, we may find ourselves asking that age old question, "Why, Lord." God isn't angered by our questions. God didn't rebuke Job for asking why. But it was through his suffering that Job learned that he didn't have all the answers he thought he had. Job came to realize that God knows more than we can ever hope to. And like a father caring for His children, He wants us to do what is best for us in the end, whether we can understand it or not. We must use hard times to strengthen our faith. Trust in the Lord, turn to Him in prayer."

Helen felt like the message was directed at her. In a way, of course, it was. It did remind her again of who was in charge. She realized that the best thing she could do was to pray. She prayed for Cindy, Janet, Jason and Marcia, for Faith and Greg and for herself that she would be able to do what God wanted her to do for this family.

Greg picked up the kids on Sundays and took them to the church they always attended which was close to their house.

Helen went to her own church and then out to eat and visit with her own children and friends.

Greg had been spending more time with the kids than he ever did before. Helen saw that he was trying to be a better father. The peace of Christ was evident in his face.

She was glad Greg took his children that Sunday. She felt kind of tired with a little headache and a tickle in her throat. "I sure hope I'm not coming down with something," she thought. She was glad she wasn't expected to cook a big meal that day.

Greg had taken the kids out for lunch after church and then to the mall for shoe shopping. Now they were relaxing in the den watching a movie.

Helen felt worse as the day went by and came back early to lay down for a while. Two hours later Janet went to check on her. Helen looked terrible. "You know, I think I may have a fever. I'm afraid I'm sick. Janet, you shouldn't be in here, I may be contagious."

"I'll be careful, Helen, you taught me how. Let me get the thermometer for you."

The thermometer confirmed Helen's suspicions. Janet went to find her dad.

"Dad, I think Helen's really sick. Her temp is up to 102. I'm not sure what to do for her."

"It's Sunday, we won't be able to get the doctor until tomorrow. I think we should call your mom. She'll know the best thing to do for tonight."

"She'll be calling any time, now," said Janet.

Twenty minutes later the phone rang. Janet answered.

"Hi, honey," her mom sounded tired.

"Hi, mom, is everything okay over there?"

Yes, it's great. I'm getting ready for bed. How is everyone?"

"I'm glad you called. I think Helen's sick. She seemed fine this morning but she took a nap after church and now she has a temperature of 102. We aren't sure what to do. Dad's here. He said to ask you."

"Well, honey, I'm sure Helen can tell you, give her some

aspirin and fluids. Watch her temperature and make sure the aspirin brings it down and call the doctor tomorrow. If the aspirin doesn't work or if her fever goes up your dad will have to take her to the hospital. Rest is the best thing for her. Don't do any hugging or get on her bed until the doctor tells you it's okay. And don't forget to wash your hand after you go in to see her. I'm sure Helen will be fine in a couple of days. Put your dad on the phone and I'll see you soon. Love you."

"Okay, mom. I love you, too."

"Don't worry, honey. Tell Jason and Cindy I'm on the phone."

"Okay. Here's dad."

"Hi, Faith. I'm glad you called, too. I guess I panicked a little bit. I'm used to you handling all these types of situations. Of course, Helen could have told us what she needs. But it's good to hear your voice. How are you? Is your project going well? Good! I think I should stay here for a few nights. Helen looks rough, Faith. It came on her fast, too. I'll call you tomorrow and let you know what the doctor says. Don't worry about a thing, I'll be here. Okay, Faith, have a good night, I love...uh, goodbye." Funny how easily we slip back into old habits, he thought.

Greg would give a lot to be able to slip back into his old life with his family. He had to believe there was a chance to try again. If he got that chance he would do a lot of things different. Maybe this was his chance. Regardless, he was here now and his kids and Helen needed him. He would face up to his responsibilities at home for once.

He still had some suits in the closet, he didn't have any of his favorite clothes at the house but it would do for tomorrow. He would have to get the kids off to school before work, leave the office early and pick something up for dinner. As Greg planned his day, he couldn't help but be happy at the prospect of spending a few days at home. Why did he ever think of buying a condo for a place to get away? This was his home in every sense of the word. His children needed him. He would be there for a few days at least. He would savor every minute of being with them.

The next day Greg took some time off of work to take Helen to the doctor who diagnosed Helen with an upper respiratory infection. He prescribed antibiotics which she took and thought she was recovering. But a week later she wasn't any better. A second visit to the doctor revealed pneumonia.

"Helen, you should really be in the hospital," he said.

"You know how I hate hospitals. I'm so anxious and uncomfortable there. I think I'd get better faster if I could stay in my own bed," she said.

"You can't stay alone, Helen. You'll need to stay in bed for a week, at least. Someone will need to take care of you, bring your meals and make sure you take your medication," he said.

The nurse walked Helen to the waiting room where Greg was waiting. "He wants me to go to the hospital," Helen said. "He says I shouldn't be alone."

"Helen, sit down before you fall down," said Greg. "The kids and I can take care of you. Heaven knows you've done it for all of us enough times."

"Oh, Greg, I can't ask you to do that," Helen said.

"You didn't ask and we won't have it any other way."

"I can't even think," Helen closed her eyes and leaned her head on the wall behind her.

"You don't have to think. I'm taking over. Nurse, is there anything else I need to do?"

"I'll have a printout of instructions sent home with you. It's true about hospitals with Helen. She will rest better at home. The doctor wants to see her back here in a week. If you have any problems just call. Feel free to use the emergency number if you need to."

Helen's illness made them all better appreciate what she did for them. There were things they all took for granted like laundry and dishes being done, and the after-school snacks which mysteriously appeared.

Dinner always seemed effortless for Helen. She never was stressed, never overwhelmed. But for Jason, Janet, and Greg, with already full schedules, it was a stretch to get everything done.

Helen tried to get up and help but the family insisted she listen to her doctor's advice.

" Okay, I'll rest for a little while. I'm sure I'll feel better tomorrow," she said.

Janet was emptying the dishwasher. Marcia was setting the table for dinner. Jason was trying to round up yesterday's laundry to put in the washer. Greg was on his way home with take-out chicken for dinner. Janet suddenly realized that she hasn't heard from Cindy in hours.

"Jason," she called upstairs.

"Yeah"

"Would you check on Cindy?"

"Yeah"

A few minutes later he rushed into the kitchen. She's not in her room. I looked everywhere upstairs and I didn't find her."

"Oh, dear Jesus," Janet had picked up some of Helen's expressions.

Janet, Jason and Marcia had found a deeper relationship through their shared faith. They were truly on the same page, literally, since they went to the same Bible study class. Little by little they were starting to worship as a family. They said a blessing at dinner, now. They went to church together with a new excitement and discussed the message on the way home. The Jones teens were on fire for Christ, trying to live their lives more like Jesus taught. So, of course, they turned to Jesus first when Cindy was missing.

"Dear Jesus, please come to our aid and help our sister. She's just a kid and she's having a hard time with everything. Be with her and with us to help us find her. In Jesus name, Amen."

In the moment of stillness that followed, they heard a voice coming from Helen's rooms. They looked at each other, then at the archway to the back hall.

They heard Cindy's voice as clear as a bell. "I'll get it, Helen, don't get up."

Janet, Marcia and Jason were looking toward Helen's rooms with their mouths open, startled expressions on their faces, just as Cindy rounded the corner. Cindy was animated and looked livelier than they had seen her in a while. She looked at them standing there with their eyes wide.

"She wants a glass of water," Cindy said.

"I can see that," said Janet. "We didn't know where you were."

"We were worried," said Jason.

"Everyone else has something important to do to help Helen," said Cindy. "And I thought maybe she might need something and I could get it for her. I came down to ask and she was thirsty. I'm getting her some water."

"Cindy are you okay?" asked Marcia. She was at a loss for words.

"I'm fine. I feel like I've been asleep for a long a time and I just woke up. I just want to help Helen. She always helps me when I need something."

"I know what you mean. Now it's our turn. I'm glad you're with us, Cindy." Janet said.

"All for one and one for all," said Jason.

"Like the four musketeers."

When Greg came home with chicken and all the trimmings, he was welcomed by laughter coming from the kitchen. For a moment he thought about what his family was going through and wondered how they could be laughing like that. And the still small voice said, "Where two or more are gathered in my name, I am there with them." His heart swelled and he joined his children encouraged by the Holy Spirit.

"Hi, kids," he said.

"Hiii, daaad," they chorused. Greg was amazed to see Cindy smiling in the kitchen but he didn't want to make a big deal about it.

"Dinner's ready. How's our patient?"

"She doesn't seem to be getting better, dad. We're making her stay in bed and rest, like the doctor said. Her fever's down but she's still so tired."

"Well, she's been through an ordeal, it's no wonder she's

tired. It'll take some time, I guess."

"I don't know, dad," said Janet. "I think you should call the doctor again. Shouldn't she be up by now?"

"I'll call her doctor and see what he says but I think we should give the anti-biotic a few more days to work. Your mom will be coming home this weekend. Hopefully things will be back to normal by then."

"Dad are you going to stay here when mom gets home?" asked Janet.

All eyes turned toward Greg, in unison.

"I don't know, honey. Right now let's just concentrate on taking care of Helen. I'll say the blessing."

"Lord, be with us in our time of need. We pray for healing for Helen and safe journey for mom. Bless this food that it may strengthen us to do your will. Amen."

Even with everything that was going on Greg couldn't help feeling grateful to be sitting here with his kids and optimistic about the future. Cindy seemed to be responding to the medication and he had formed a closer bond with Jason and Janet, united by more than genes. Marcia seemed like one of the kids. The aphorism was true, he was gaining a daughter instead of losing a son.

While they were cleaning up the dinner dishes Janet said, "Dad, did you notice this weekend is Valentine's Day?"

"You're right, it is."

"I think you should do something for mom."

"Oh, honey, I don't know. I don't want to be too pushy."

"You want to do something for her, don't you?"

"Yes, of course."

"If you do something without expecting something in return, that's not pushy, is it?"

"How'd you get so smart?"

Janet smiled.

CHAPTER 16

Homecoming

Faith arrived at the airport late at night. She was exhausted. No one was waiting for her and she took a taxi home. When she saw her home she felt some of her stress leave her. She stumbled up to the house knowing that she wouldn't have been able to make it much further. When she finally walked in the door it was like being wrapped in a warm blanket on a cold day.

A few small lights had been left on for her. She put her suitcase in the foyer instead of dragging it up the steps and noticed roses on the table. On the way past the dining room she glanced in and saw roses on the dining room table. And when she looked in the living room she saw roses on the coffee table and a large lumpy shape on the couch. That would be Greg, she sighed to herself.

Her anger was subsiding a little. She knew their marriage was over. Faith also knew that Greg had been spending a lot of time at home helping with Helen's illness, taking care of the house and kids and going to church with them on Sunday. It didn't really have anything to do with her. He was the one who chose to live a separate life from her. He broke his promise of a faithful life together. And he humiliated her in front of everyone. People at work in the states treated her like a poor widow and in a way she guessed she was. At least in France no one knew, or maybe they didn't care. She hadn't established any friendships there, kept all dealings at a business level.

All Faith wanted was to turn off her thoughts and sink into oblivion. Maybe if she could get some rest she would feel more like herself. She climbed the stairs, one agonizing step at a time. She kicked off her shoes and finally got onto her own bed. For a few moments she felt the relief of relaxing muscles. Then, unwanted thoughts invaded as if someone had hit the "on" switch. Scenes flashed through her mind of Greg downstairs on the couch, Greg smiling at Amanda at some office party. Jason holding a crying baby, Cindy curled in a ball, unresponsive. Helen in a Hospital, her home in chaos, the house a mess. She had no idea what she would find in the morning. The kids were putting up a brave front for her sake, she was sure. "How could anyone be this tired and still be awake?" she thought. Faith could not remember ever being so sad and depressed.

In the pre-dawn hours Faith Jones came to the end of herself. She realized she didn't make Greg cheat on her, Marcia pregnant, Helen sick or Cindy depressed. Her life was in ruins, her dreams were destroyed and she had no control over any of it.

In her mind she cried out to God. "Lord, how did I get so lost? How could this happen to us? What am I going to do? I can't fix this. I need you, Lord. Forgive me. I've been selfish and prideful. I made decisions about my life and my family based only on what I want. How did I forget I don't have any control over any of this?"

"I remember when you were the most important thing in my life. We were all so happy. When did it become all about me again? Oh, Jesus, is it too late? With everything that happened to my family and my commitment to work, can I ever have that peace again? And a thought, clear and pure, came to Faith, "With men this is impossible but with God all things are possible." She felt her muscles relax, her tension ease in the peace of the Spirit which surpasses all understanding. With tears on her cheeks and "thank you, Jesus" on her lips, she slipped into the oblivion she had so desperately sought.

Faith awoke to the sound of her family and the smell of coffee and cinnamon toast. Her heart felt lighter than it had yesterday even as she regained consciousness and the realization of her situation. She opened her eyes and looked toward the door surprised to see Cindy peeking in.

"Mom," Cindy bounded into the room and onto the bed. "I couldn't wait to see you. Daddy's here and we're making breakfast and Jason and Marcia are here. Marcia has a baby in her belly. She's my cousin. And Helen's going to be okay. Why do you have a skirt on?"

Faith was astonished by Cindy's speech. It was the most she had heard Cindy say in a very long time. And what she was saying was so positive. Cindy was happy and excited about the same things that had overwhelmed Faith and brought her to the brink of despair.

"Come here, honey," said Faith.

Cindy curled up next to her mom.

"I've missed you. How are you doing?"

"I woke up. I think I was sleeping for a long time. I had bad dreams and I was sad. But I woke up."

Here was her sweet Cindy, all smile and curls like she used to be. Faith put her arms around her daughter and held her. Faith remembered her epiphany of last night. It was amazing how different her circumstances seemed today. Just remembering that she had very little control over the future and absolutely no control over the past was liberating. Being home, where the problems were and being part of them made Faith feel hope that everything might be okay. A passage from the Bible, "For we do not wrestle against flesh and blood, but against powers, against the rulers of the darkness of this age, against spiritual hosts of wickedness in the heavenly places." Faith wondered if this was one of those moments where there was only one set of footprints in the sand.

Faith looked around her bedroom. The sun was bright and there were roses on the dresser. Didn't I see roses in the foyer, dining room, and living room last night, she thought? Jason and

Janet walked in carrying a tray of cinnamon toast, fruit, juice and coffee before she could formulate a theory about the appearance of roses.

"We figured you were up when Cindy didn't come back down" said Janet. "We brought you breakfast. I'm so glad you're home."

"I'm glad I'm home, too. Breakfast looks great, guys. Thanks. Okay, tell me everything. Cindy filled me in on a lot of what's going on, Faith smiled at her youngest daughter and gave her a squeeze. How's Helen?"

Janet spoke first, "I don't know, mom." I thought the pills the doctor gave her should have made her better by now. I never knew anyone who was sick this long except Aunt Katie and she had cancer. I'm worried but dad said to wait a few days. She doesn't seem to be worse, but she's still sleeping a lot."

"I think she's better this morning. She's not coughing as much," Jason said. "She had toast and juice for breakfast. She said she was going to get up and take a shower."

"I've been helping, "said Cindy, "I get her things so she doesn't have to get up,"

"I'm sure Helen really appreciates your help. I'm so proud of you, Cindy. And I'm glad you woke up because we all missed you."

"I miss you, too, mommy." She reached up and put her arms around Faith's neck.

"Will you two give us a few minutes, Please?" she looked at Jason and Janet," I'm going to get a shower and get dressed and I'll be down soon, OK?"

"Yeah, mom," they said in perfect unison.

"By the way, where did all the roses come from? Asked Faith.

Janet and Jason looked at each other.

"From daddy, "said Cindy.

Anger welled up in Faith threatening her newly regained sense of peace.

Janet saw the changed of expression on her mother's face and knew her father had been right about not wanting to be pushy.

"It was my idea, mom," she rushed to explain. Janet told the story of how the roses came to be there.

Faith's mouth was pursed with anger but her eyes mirrored the pain in her heart.

"Janet, I don't think it's appropriate," she said.

"It's not like he gave them to you, mom. He put flowers in every room for Valentine's Day. You know, like decoration. Dads changed a lot, mom. I'm not defending him, but you could give him a chance. You're always telling me to keep an open mind. That's all I'm saying. A lot has changed around here. It's all good, mom. Just look at Cindy."

"Yes, look at Cindy," Faith smiled at her youngest daughter and gave her a hug. "I'll see you and Jason downstairs in a few minutes.

On the way down the stairs Jason said, "Did you notice something a little different about mom. The last time I saw her she looked like she was about to crack."

"Yep, no doubt. I can't wait to hear what happened. I'm not sure she's ready to see dad, though. She looks so tired."

"You might be right."

Helen, Greg and Marcia were in the kitchen when Jason and Janet walked in. Jason walked over to give Marcia a side hug. She looked very happy and very pregnant.

"Helen, what are you doing up" asked Janet.

"I can't lie in that bed any longer. I'm feeling a little better. I won't get my strength back unless I start moving around and eating something. I thought I'd make eggs for breakfast. Who wants some?"

Tell you what," said Marcia, "you sit right here and have some orange juice and I'll make the eggs. How do you like them?"

Marcia's maternal instincts were kicking in lately. Jason was looking at her in complete adoration. The two of them were almost always together these days.

"Dad, you were right about being pushy with the flowers. I told mom it was my idea. She looked mad. It might be better if you weren't here when she comes down."

"You're probably right, honey. I don't want to upset her. I have to go to the office anyway. I'll call later."

As Greg drove away from his home he felt the cold emptiness filling his soul again. Nothing he'd done had helped. His being there while she was off in France wasn't even acknowledged. He'd taken care of the kids, the house and Helen. He'd delegated some of his own work at the office to do it. He'd helped pull his family together these past two weeks. And then Faith came home and he was tossed aside. What about HIS feelings?

All at once Greg recognized the old pattern of thinking had resurfaced. He pulled over to the side of the road, closed his eyes and opened his heart once again to his Heavenly Father.

"Please Father, I don't want to go there again. Help me to be understanding of my families' needs right now. I know you are in control. I know you want what's best for us. Please be with us in this time of trial, that we may do Your will for Your glory. Thank you, Lord, for all Your blessings and the chance last week to reconnect with my kids and be there for them. Please be with Faith and bring my family back together. I know I don't deserve it but I ask in Jesus' name. Amen."

Faith held her youngest daughter close in mutual affection. She could tell that Cindy needed support and in truth, so did she. Just holding Cindy, knowing that she was doing better, was like the proverbial island in a storm; a glimpse of positive that can come from negative. A hope for a bright future for all of them, regardless of the hardships or maybe even because of them.

Faith and Cindy went downstairs and found her family in the kitchen, all except Greg, she thought with mixed feelings. Marcia was making scrambled eggs and Faith joined Helen, Janet and Jason at the island chatting. Faith felt relaxed in a way that she realized she hadn't felt in a long time. They all sat at the kitchen island and thanked God for the food, Faith's safe trip home and Helen's improved health.

After the meal Helen went back to her room to lie down. Faith and the kids were watching a movie, Faith was still tired and was so happy that she didn't have to spend the day cleaning and doing laundry. You guys are amazing. I always knew you had it in you but this just proves how capable and grown up you are."

Cindy said, "I helped, too. I took care of Helen. I read to her and got her water and things. And I kept my room cleaned up. And let Janet and Jason tell me what to do without arguing."

Janet and Jason exchanged glances and smiles. Cindy had been helping but often under protest. They both knew instinctively how important praise was for her right now.

"And she helped put the dishes away and put her own laundry away. Tell mom about your test."

"I got an A+ on my language arts test."

"Oh, Cindy, I'm so proud of you."

"And I'm going to gymnastics. I didn't want to go back. I thought the kids would laugh at me, again. But they were all glad to see me. Coach says not to get so serious about it and just have fun. I like it that way."

"I think your coach is a very smart man," said Faith.

"He is."

"I can't tell you how proud I am of all of you. I suddenly see you in a new light. Part of that may be that I reconnected with Jesus last night. I need His help to get through this. I know you both had a similar experience a couple of months ago, so you can understand how I feel."

They joined together in a group hug. Faith bowed her head to lead them in prayer, her cheek resting on the top of Cindy's head. "Lord, thank you for your presence and help in bringing us together. Help us do your will through these difficult times. In Jesus name we pray. Amen."

CHAPTER 17

Counselor

The end of February was mild and March started out beautiful. The Jones family fell into a pattern and as spring came with its rainy days and new growth, the whole family felt their spirits uplifted. It looked like it would be a nice long spring.

Faith had hired a local French woman to help her with the project overseas. With the help of her phone and computer she was able to spend two weeks in France and two weeks at home.

Sophie was her eyes and ears. The plans had already been made and construction crews were at work. Sophie seemed to understand exactly what Faith was trying to achieve. She knew most of the men and commanded their respect, the result of her open, honest, rather loud and boisterous personality. It was comical to see those large macho men turn almost sheepish in the presence of one of her scolding's. She would laugh with them just as readily.

When Faith was home she spent a good part of her day on her phone and computer. With a six-hour time difference, it was a challenge. Sometimes the phone would ring at three or four in the morning for Faith to troubleshoot situations that couldn't wait. She was the only link to the board who provided approval for changes and financing.

Greg had been staying at the house with Helen and the kids when Faith was overseas. The decision was made by mutual consent and the needs of the children. Faith got home late one Saturday night to find Greg asleep on the couch in the den. In the morning he started getting ready for church which had become routine. He wasn't sure how to handle the situation, knowing that Faith was still understandably resentful and barely tolerated his presence, for the sake of the kids.

It was as if they were going through the motions but with a wall between them. Communication was at a most basic level and emotions kept under tight control. One thing that linked them was their shared faith in Christ. There was no denying that the Holy Spirit had been at work in this family. Each one of them looked forward to church on Sunday so and on this beautiful Sunday in March the Jones Family entered their church together. Maybe their family wasn't healed but this was a big step toward that goal, whether they all realized it or not.

They sat together in church, the children between them. It wasn't that Faith wanted to sit with him. But the kids walked in and sat down beside him, she could either sit with her family or sit by herself. She was aware of the gossip going on in the church about them. She wondered if Pastor David had noticed, too, as his sermon was from Matthew 7:1-3, "Judge not that you be not judged. For with what judgement you judge, you will be judged; and with the measure you use, it will be measured back to you. And why do you look at the speck in your brothers' eye but do not consider the plank in your own eye?"

The words of Jesus rang true for her on so many levels. Wasn't she being judged? Those people didn't know what was really going on. Wasn't she judging Greg? But he deserved it didn't he? It was so confusing.

During the week, Alice called and invited her out for lunch. They met at a quaint café after the lunch rush and sat in a quiet corner. They talked about their jobs, the flowers in church and the kids.

"I'm going to come right out and say it," Alice said.

"Okay, say it."

"How long are you going to make that man suffer for what he did?"

"If he's suffering, it's not because of me."

"Oh, no? Do you know what he does every time you go back to France? He's over at your house helping the kids with homework, taking Cindy to practice; he's even hosted the youth group. He's been leaving the office earlier. He's been delegating a lot of what he used to take on by himself. Roger said he was commended by the board for efficiency and teamwork. Their whole department is running smoother than ever."

"I'm sure he and Amanda make a good team."

"Haven't you heard? She quit months ago. Greg isn't seeing anyone." Alice said.

"Faith, I'm sorry I didn't tell you about Greg and Amanda when I found out. All I knew was what Roger said and he wasn't really sure. I didn't want to hurt you over a maybe. I'm not saying what he did was okay, Faith. But you should think about putting it behind you and moving on. I think he's really changed."

"That's so unfair, Alice. I was the one who go hurt, remember. He's a cheat and a liar. People don't just all of the sudden lose their bad qualities. Sure, he's acting like the devoted husband and father right now. He's even got people feeling sorry for him, obviously."

"I'm not saying it'll be easy to forgive him. It may take a long time to learn to trust him again."

"I'm not sure I can do that."

"So what are you going to do? Give up the life you made together? Get a divorce and divide your children?"

"We haven't made any decisions like that. I don't know what I want to do."

"Look, all I'm saying is that you can't keep going like this. It's hard on the kids and it's hard on Greg."

"So what? Don't you think he deserves it? It's not like I

kicked him out of his home entirely. And it's not like he doesn't have another home to go to. He has his "love nest", doesn't he?" Faith felt the anger seething inside her.

"Have you thought about counseling? There's a great Christian counselor and he's a member of the church."

"Oh, come on, Alice. What could a counselor possibly tell me that I don't already know?"

You would have to go and find out, Faith. But I do know that your family is suffering. It's below the surface, now, but it's still there. Even if you don't want to do it for yourself or for Greg, you should think about doing it for the kids, especially Cindy. I don't know if it'll help, but it can't hurt, right?"

"To what end, Alice? You mean to sit down in a room with a total stranger and talk about why I should go out of my way to forgive him and go back to the way things used to be? Why would I want that? I don't like way things used to be, especially the part about cheating and lying."

"I think Greg would do just about anything to turn this thing around."

"How could I ever trust him again? Why should I even try, Alice. I don't think I even love him anymore. And I don't need him."

"For your kids, Faith, for your marriage and for you. It's not like you to avoid an issue."

Faith knew her friend was right. She hated unsolved problems.

"I guess you're right. I need to face this head on. I need to face Greg. Better to do it with a referee. Who's this counselor you're talking about? I have to do something; I guess it couldn't hurt to talk to him."

Greg agreed to go to the marriage counselor. They waited three weeks for an appointment with Dr. Mason. Faith had been to France and back. When she was forced to be in the same room as Greg, she avoided eye contact and didn't speak to him unless it was necessary. She was anxious about the meeting with the counselor and Greg. She wasn't looking forward to facing him but she did want some kind of spoken agreement about how they were going to proceed.

Faith had asked about privacy when she learned Dr. Mason's office was in his home. Dr. Mason assured her that his office was sound proofed to protect his client's privacy. Faith didn't know if the debate that was sure to result from this meeting would become heated.

Faith and Greg arrived at the large three-story Victorian at the same time.

"Hi, Faith, I really appreciate this chance." Greg said.

"Don't thank me, Greg. It makes me feel like I'm giving you something and frankly, I don't think you deserve it." She returned.

"I agree."

They both looked miserable when the housekeeper answered the door.

"Mr. and Mrs. Jones? Follow me, please." She led them to a large room just past the entryway.

The door opened on a huge room with a beautiful fireplace. The large mantel had an antique clock on it with an English landscape suspended above it. In front of the fireplace there was a comfortable grouping of chairs that seemed to invite the observer to sit. To the left was a picture window with a mahogany desk in front of it, positioned so the person sitting at the desk would be looking out of the window. To the right of the room was a table and chairs.

In a few minutes Dr. Mason entered to find the Jones couple on opposite sides of the room looking away from each other.

"Mr. and Mrs. Jones, welcome. I want a good clean fight. Please enter the ring and shake hands."

It was such an unexpected thing to hear that neither of them could stop the chuckle that escaped.

"Now, there, that broke the ice. I'm Dr. Mason, he shook their hands. I like to start each session with a prayer. Would that be okay with both of you?"

"Yes, thank you, doctor," said Faith.

"I appreciate it," said Greg.

Lord, we humbly ask you to be here with us while we try to sort things out. We believe your word which says, when two or more are gathered in My Name, I am there with them. Guide our thoughts, let us be led by you in all we say and do now and forever, Amen."

"First, I'd like you to tell me a little about yourselves. I'd like to know you better and Olga, the housekeeper, will be in here with tea in a couple of minutes. No amount of persuading can make her stop serving tea to guests. She says she won't have any part of such rudeness. She's one in a million."

Immediately, as if on cue, there was a light tap on the door and in came Olga with tea, little cucumber sandwiches and strawberry tarts.

They all tanked Olga and sat on the group of chairs in front of the fireplace.

"Doctor, I appreciate your hospitality," said Faith. I was very nervous about coming here. I'm feeling much better about it now."

"Thank you and I'm glad. Mr. Jones, may I know your frame of mind?"

"This is all very nice, doctor, but the reason for our being here is not. Let's talk about the hard stuff, why don't we?" said Greg.

"Okay, why don't you tell me what on your mind, Greg."

"I've been waiting for the opportunity to ask Faith for forgiveness. Faith, I am sorrier than I can say. I know I don't deserve this chance. That's what I was trying to say outside, Faith. Thanks."

"Let me put my cards on the table," Faith said. "I don't think I'm in line with God's will on this because when he says that to me it just makes me angry. I don't want to do anything he would thank me for."

Okay, what I'm seeing here is a wife who is hurt and angry

and a husband who is sorry. Would you both say that's a correct assessment?" They both nodded.

If you don't mind, Faith, I'd like to hear what Greg has to say first."

"That doesn't seem quite fair," she said.

"I have my reasons, Faith. It would be better if you just listen for now, as an observer. Try to be as objective as possible as if you were an audience watching a play."

Greg told the doctor about his indiscretions. He told how long it had been going on. He talked for a long time. He had decided to be brutally honest. If there were a possibility of saving his marriage it would be with the truth.

He glanced at Faith from time to time. She was sitting with her legs crossed, staring at her hands folded in her lap.

Greg told about Christmas morning and his choice to try to live in the will of God. "Nothing's been the same since then. It's so amazing that Jason and Janet accepted Christ a couple of months before I did. It's brought our relationship to a different level."

When Greg stopped talking the doctor asked Faith, "How do you see the situation?"

Faith looked up. "I had no idea it was going on all this time," she said. "I must be some kind of idiot. And now you say everything is different and you've given your life to Christ? I thought you'd done that long ago, Greg. How can you expect me to believe you? You may have your children fooled but it will take a lot more to convince me, if it's even possible."

She looked back at Dr. Mason. "The part that bothers me most, doctor, is that I am lost in this anger. I also had a re-awakening, a reconnection with Christ. For that moment everything was clear to me, I felt peaceful. I knew everything was going to be okay. But it didn't last. After what Greg just said, I'm not sure I can find that peace again. I wasn't sure I could ever forgive his having an affair. How can I possibly continue in a marriage based on lies?"

"I wish I could say something to fix it but as Christians we know only God can do that. Sometimes an objective observer can see things the people involved can't. Do you think it's a coincidence that your whole family found help in Christ, separately but within months of each other? What amazing timing this is, miraculous I would say. Some day when the sin is far in the past and the pain and hurt are all gone God will still be there with you. My advice is from Philippians 4:6-8, 'Be anxious for nothing, but in everything by prayer and supplication, with thanksgiving, let your requests be made known to God; and the peace of God, which surpasses all understanding, will guard your hearts and minds through Christ Jesus. Finally, brethren, whatever things are true, whatever things are noble, whatever things are just, whatever things are pure, whatever things are lovely, whatever things are of good report, if there is any virtue and if there is anything praiseworthy – meditate on these things."

While thanking God for things you could add the blessing of your children. Children are always a gift from God and it sounds like you have very special kids. I have seen them at church, of course, but I'd like to meet them sometime. They are our hope for the future. I can see God at work in the family, big time."

They talked about the kids, the changes they had all been through. Somehow they had both managed to spend more time at home and their jobs hadn't suffered. In fact, by delegating responsibility there was more input and less stress.

For a moment, when they were talking about their work and what they were both doing, respectively, to have more time at home, Greg felt a spark of the friendship they had once shared. He looked at Faith and smile.

Faith's walls went up immediately, protecting her shattered heart. Greg saw it in her eyes and hung his head. The doctor merely held one of each of their hands and said, "Let us pray. Dear Lord, you see before you two of Your dear children, broken and confused. We are so grateful to you, Father, for your many blessings. You have poured out such love on this family and for that may we all be truly grateful. In your Holy Name we pray. Amen."

"Amen," said Faith.

"Amen," echoed Greg.

Our time is up but you both have homework," said the doctor.

"Homework?" Greg and Faith asked un unison.

Dr. Mason smiled. "You both have already done so much to alleviate the situation by turning to Christ, by changing your priorities and by coming here. I truly do see God at work in your family and I am awed by it. So, your homework is to meditate on good things. Allow negative thoughts but try to look at them objectively. When you have a thought or emotion that you don't want, allow it to play out and say, "that's interesting." These thoughts are part of you and in that way they are important. Allow them, embrace them, but don't let them have any power over your actions. I think you're both already doing this unconsciously, I want you to be aware of it. Balance these thoughts with thoughts of being grateful or any thought that brings peace. Keep a journal, it'll be helpful in the future.

If you haven't already done it, set aside a quiet time to pray and read your Bibles each day. How long isn't as important right now as the depth of your prayer. Connect with Him every day.

Jesus told us while He was here on earth that 'You shall love the Lord your God with all your heart, with all your soul and with all your mind.' Matthew 22:37

Faith, if you focus on Him it will help alleviate your anger. Keep a song on your lips and a prayer in your heart. Satan loves it when we stay angry. It is a poison for your soul. Jesus was very specific on this subject. It's a hard assignment but it is paramount for your own health and the happiness in your family.

Greg, your poison is, of course, your guilt. When you were saved you became a new person in Christ, washed clean because He paid the price for our sins. That's an incredible thing. He erases our sin, but not the consequences. God does, however, give us the grace to handle those consequences. Stay in prayer in in line with Gods will. Healing is already happening in your family, more than you know.

Now, return to your corners."

Greg and Faith both chuckled again, said their goodbyes and went on their way, both strangely refreshed. The idea of having something positive to work on appealed to both of them.

Everything was quiet when Faith walked in her front door. She heard humming coming from the kitchen and headed that direction.

"Hi, Helen, how are you feeling?" said Faith.

"Right as rain. I still get tired more easily than normal but I suspect it's temporary. I've been meaning to talk to you about that check. I don't feel right about being paid for being sick. I didn't do anything to earn it; in fact you all took care of me.

Don't be silly, Helen. You earned it and more. I know things have been hard around here lately. I've never once heard you complain. You're always there for all of us. It's my way of showing you how much you're appreciated. Whether you're sick or well."

"Thanks, Faith." Helen was moved. "How did your appointment go?"

"The doctor was nice. His house is beautiful. Greg and I both got things off our chest. We said things that normally would have led to an argument but didn't because there was a referee. I guess it went well all things considered. He gave us homework. We're supposed to stay in the word and meditate on good things. I'm glad we went to a Christian counselor. After all, it'll take a miracle to save this marriage." Faith said.

She was thinking about a marriage based on lies and how many women Greg had been with. He's been lying to her all along. It was a nice thought to walk in the Grace of God and get past her anger. She just wasn't sure it was possible. And the clear, quiet thought "with God all things are possible" came to mind.

Helen saw the tears form in Faiths eyes, spill over and slide down her cheeks. She put her arms around the grieving woman and said, "It's going to be okay. I can feel the Lord at work here."

"That's what the doctor said. It must be true. But I can't figure out what God could do to make it okay. It's not like the past can be erased. I wish I could think about something else; I feel like

I need a break from my feelings. I'm just tired, I think. I'm actually looking forward to getting back to France and back to work."

"Everything is going to be just fine, Faith. I believe what James says in the Bible about trials bringing us closer to God. The proof is all around us."

"Thank you, Helen, for everything you do."

CHAPTER 18

Decisions

F aith looked forward to going to France but once there she worried about her family at home. She was torn between her love and devotion to her family and the project in France which felt personal to her at this point. This project was very likely a turning point in her career and she felt very lucky to have been given this chance and responsibility. She was determined to do her best.

She felt an amazing sense of accomplishment for her work. At the same time there was disquiet in her heart. She was homesick and she knew she was not in Gods will. What had she been thinking getting involved with a project like this when her family needed her so much? A commitment had been made to the club, but she wondered if she was being fair to them, to her family and to herself. While she didn't want to live a life centered on herself, she knew balance was important. How do you balance the needs of your family, your job, God's desire for your life and still be true to your own desires? She didn't know what the answer was. Anything she did would let someone down.

She was separated from her family whether she was at home in the states or at her house in France. When she was home her family knew that she would be leaving and the feeling of separation was tangible. It seemed no matter where she was, someone was suffering from her absence. Her thoughts and emotions were spinning out of control, another indication that she wasn't in line with Gods will. She prayed often for God to take control of her life and lead her. She reminded herself of the circumstances last year which brought her once again to her savior. She was determined not to lose her way again. She knew it is often a trial that brings us back to Christ and she didn't want another trial.

Her confusion had started on Christmas when she woke up in Greg's arms. Greg had come over to spend Christmas Eve with the kids. The tradition in their family was that in the afternoon of Christmas Eve, they had an open house party and friends dropped by to wish each other Merry Christmas. This year they decided to continue with the tradition not only for the kid's sake but to assure their friends that even though their family was going through difficult times, they were okay. The party also helped dissuade the gossip they knew was circulating in their community.

In the evening, after everyone left, they had eggnog and watched Christmas movies. It was a special time for all of them because no matter what was going on in their life, Christmas Eve was one of the few times that family was a priority. Last year they had spent Christmas apart. This year each member of the Jones family appreciated being together as they never had before. It was close to midnight when the kids finally went to bed and more importantly, fell asleep so that Greg and Faith could do the Santa Clause part. Afterwards, they sat on either end of the couch absorbed in their own thoughts. White Christmas was playing on the TV, the fire was starting to go out, the Christmas lights made the den look like a fairyland. The moment was rather awkward and at the same time familiar and comforting and neither wanted to be alone. They had fallen asleep and apparently had turned to each other in their sleep, Faith's head on his shoulder and Greg's arm around her.

For a moment, when they awoke, it seemed like everything was as it should be. As consciousness took over, the reality of the situation and the emotions attached to it rushed in like a wave. Christmas Day for Faith was like walking in a fog. Sometimes she thought of the love and friendship they had shared over the years. They were stronger as a team. They saw eye to eye on most things and had learned to compromise when they didn't. She missed his support and his strength of character. Greg helped her be a better person.

But her marriage had been an illusion. Greg's strength of character was only on the surface. Underneath he was a cheat, a weak man who had destroyed her trust in him. Faith pushed away the memories of what she had considered a perfect marriage, nothing was left to her but betrayal.

Now here she was in France again, unsure how to proceed with her life. She tried to lose herself in the responsibilities of her work and from time to time she did. But she always came back to the reality of her situation. Her own guilt reminded her she had walked out on her family. How could I have ever thought a decision like this made sense?

She followed Dr. Masons advice and prayed for help every morning and said a prayer of gratitude in the evening. Somehow, though, Faith didn't feel that deep connection with God until one night when she couldn't seem to find anything to be grateful for.

"What can I do, God? What do you expect me to do? I can't just leave France and walk out on this job. Lord, please take control of my life. Fix it for me that I can live in Your will." And the still small voice said, "My Grace is sufficient for you, for My strength is made perfect in weakness." With the words of the Holy Spirit came the peace Faith sought. Every day she sought it and every day she was blessed. But the situation remained. She lived between two worlds, essentially two lives. She was dedicated to both; both needed her full-time undivided attention."

Faith learned to live one day at a time, doing her best to accomplish what she needed to that day and not worry too much about things outside of her control. She started to understand Greg's commitment to his job all these years, and the guilt he must have felt for him to missing out on so much going on in the family. She came to a deeper appreciation of the capabilities of her family. They were all stepping up to the plate in her absence and she respected each one in a new way.

The Lord was working in her, she realized. He was changing her life but not in the way she had expected. God was changing her priorities, not her circumstances. That was still up to her. She had to do something about the situation. Things couldn't keep going the way they were. She decided to talk to Janeen and tell her how she felt. Janeen had always seemed like an understanding person.

She called Janeen the next day for their weekly meeting. After they finished talking about work Faith asked if she could schedule an appointment with her when she came back to the states to talk about a personal matter.

"What's up, Faith?" asked Janeen. "Is there any reason why we can't talk about it right now?"

"Well, no. I had thought we could talk in person but if you have time I guess now is okay," said Faith.

"I've got time. Shoot."

"I've been thinking that it may be time for me to come back to the states."

"What are you saying?"

"I'm saying that I think this project can get along without me. I'm concerned that my family can't"

"How can you say that? You ARE this project. I expected more from you than this. You aren't the type to quit."

"I'm not saying I want to quit, Janeen. I'm saying that at this stage the only thing required is to be able to follow the blueprints and then the decorator will take over. I want some time at home, a few months at least."

"You're home half of the month now. In my experience a project like this suffers when the manager is absent,."

"Sophia can be my eyes. She already manages the

employees. She's been invaluable. I can oversee from home. I've been doing that half the time anyway. It seems to work just fine."

"What will you do? Play stay at home mom?"

"To be honest, Janeen, my home life is in turmoil. Greg and I are in counseling and my kids need me. I feel like I ran to France to escape and now I need to invest some time in my family. I can come to the office every day if you prefer. I wouldn't suggest it if I didn't think it would work."

It took so long for Janeen to respond that Faith started getting worried. She had a brief thought of what her life would be like without a job. And then Janeen spoke," To be honest, you have been missed around here. We may be able to work something out. Let me think about it. I'll talk to the CEO and let you know. He may want to bring it to the board. I'm glad you talked to me about it. I'm aware of what your family is going through and I agree that family is the most important thing."

Faith was speechless. She had been sure Janeen would be upset. She took a deep breath and thanked Janeen. Relief started unknotting her muscles soon after she hung up. She decided not to tell the kids about the conversation with her boss until a decision was made.

Faith had waited her whole life for an opportunity to work overseas like this. Now, it didn't seem so important. Jason and Marcia would be having a baby, soon. She was going to be a grandmother. Her little Cindy was coming to life. Janet seemed to have matured overnight.

And then there was Greg. She remembered the love they once had. She longed for the security and closeness their family had once shared. They had been to the counselor several times and Greg swore that God had changed him.

Beneath the anger and resentment, Faith wished it were true. She longed for her family to be together again, just like it used to be. No, that relationship was a lie. She prayed daily for help and guidance.

CHAPTER 19

Foregiveness

I t's important to know what you expect to accomplish at these meetings," Dr Mason said. "We need to set your goals and make sure we're all on the same page."

Greg spoke up, "I'd like to think there's a chance that we can be a family again."

That one simple statement opened the faucets in Faith's eyes. Her thoughts were in turmoil. She couldn't imagine ever having intimate family moments with him again. She couldn't imagine not having them. Yes, it was time for a decision. She needed to get it together, but how?

"I don't know if that's possible for me, Greg."

"Then why are we here? I thought you wanted to work through this."

"Why don't we talk about what we lost? We lost our friendship; I certainly don't want to be friends with a cheat. We lost our whole way of life. I lost respect and trust for my husband." By now tears were streaming down her cheeks. She looked so hurt and so vulnerable.

Dr Mason intervened, "That's good. We've established that Greg wants to come home. Faith, you need some more time before you can make a decision. That's understandable. What I'd like to know is why you're here?"

"I needed to do something and I didn't know what." Faith sobbed.

"I'm going to go out on a limb here, Faith. You tell me if I'm barking up the wrong tree."

Faith smiled at him through her tears. Dr. Mason's use of cliché diffused her emotions.

"I want to say that if you wanted to give up on your marriage, you wouldn't have chosen to come to counseling. Further, if you didn't want to work through this using Christian principles, you wouldn't have come to me. Faith, biblically you have every right to a divorce. But if you want to keep your family together, it can be done."

"To what end, doctor? To live with someone you don't trust, always wondering who they're with. To be resentful and suspicious? I can't live that way." Faith's expression had hardened.

There's no easy solution, but many couples work through this. They often come to a deeper understanding of each other and a happier, healthier marriage. Remember 2 Corinthians 12:9 'And he said unto me, My Grace is sufficient for thee: for my strength is made perfect in weakness.' I've seen it happen many times."

Dr. Mason had no way of knowing what meaning that passage had to Faith.

"I don't know what to say other than what I already said, I just don't know," she said. "You're telling me you think I should just get past all of this and build a stronger marriage because my husband's been skirting around behind my back all this time?"

"No, Faith, I don't know what's best for you and Greg. I'm trying to give you options, remind you of biblical principles. I do council getting past it. Lingering resentment is poison to our body, mind and soul."

"I appreciate what you're saying, doctor. I need some time.

Can we talk about this next time?"

"Yes, certainly. Our time's almost up, anyway. I'd like to say an old but in my mind a powerful prayer, to close."

They joined hands.

"May the Lord bless you and keep you. May the Lord make his face to shine upon you and give you peace. Amen."

As they shook hands goodbye, Dr. Mason handed them each a bookmark for their bible. "You can never have enough of these," he said.

"Thank you, doctor," said Faith.

"See you next time," Greg looked miserable. He hadn't said much.

Faith forgot about the bookmark until the next day when she opened her Bible and read, "seeds of discouragement can't take root in a grateful heart." Dr. Mason seemed to know how she was feeling. Maybe she shouldn't be so quick to dismiss his counsel. Her reading for the day was from Galatians 5:22, "The fruit of the Spirit is love, joy, peace, longsuffering, kindness, goodness, faithfulness, gentleness, self-control." How she longed for a life like that. Faith prayed that somehow God would take away some of her anger. But when she thought about it she realized that she wasn't quite as preoccupied with it as she had been. She was exhausted, but not as angry.

As time passed and her anger subsided she began to miss her husband. She couldn't trust him, couldn't believe what he said. But she could trust Jesus. If Greg had really given his heart to Christ, their relationship couldn't be the same. Priorities were different; love itself would be bound through Him who is love.

As Faith was reading her Bible that day she came across a verse she had heard many times before. This time it spoke to her heart and she knew, without a doubt, what God wanted her to do. "Love is patient, love is kind. It does not envy, it does not boast, it is not proud. It does not dishonor others, it is not self-seeking, it is not easily angered, it keeps no record of wrong. Love does not delight in evil but rejoices with the truth. It always protects, always trusts, always hopes, always perseveres."

She had no idea how to start. She could try to stay close to God but what was next? What practical step could she take?

Faith was glad she and Greg were still seeing Dr. Mason. The only thing she could think of to do was to bring up her thoughts in counseling.

Greg's eyes held hope when she brought the subject up of reconciliation at their next session.

"I know I don't deserve your forgiveness or another chance," he said. "I'll do whatever you need me to, Faith. I don't expect you to believe me and trust me, now. But I want you to know, I love you, Faith, I always have."

"I don't understand how you could have done it. But I know that I love you, too, Greg. I miss our family. I miss our life – the life I thought we had. I'm just not sure what to do about it. Nothing can ever be the same between us, that much is certain."

"I want to come home, Faith. I'll sleep in the spare room. I want to show you that I am a new man in Christ, give Him a chance to heal our marriage," Greg said.

"I don't think I'm ready for that, Greg."

Dr. Mason said, "Is it something you would like to set as a goal?"

"I think so," she said. "I need to take this slow."

"How would you like to proceed?" he asked.

"Why don't we try spending time together without the kids?"

"Do you mean like a date?" asked Greg.

"Yes."

And with that Greg and Faith started on the road to recovery. The walls Faith had built around her heart had started to come down. It was almost painful and yet liberating.

Faith prayed for help in being able to forgive Greg. She knew she had to, but how? When she thought about forgiving him the offenses kept coming up. She went to see Dr. Mason.

"Faith, I understand your dilemma," Dr. Mason said. "I can't tell you what you should do, but I can counsel you on forgiveness. If you're forgiving Greg to prove you're better than he is, it is not true forgiveness. And if you're doing it just because you think you should, it won't release you from resentment. If you want to be a martyr, accept the pain and hurt and set Greg free, well, Faith, that won't work either. Real forgiveness requires that you see him as a valuable person who messed up. It doesn't take away his sin, only Christ can do that. Forgiveness says that you're willing to put Greg's infidelity in the past and proceed into the future.

"How will I ever be able to trust him again," she asked.

"There are never any guarantees. The very nature of trust requires the possibility of being hurt."

Greg moved into the spare room the next weekend. He put the condo up for sale immediately. He never wanted to see it again. It represented a part of his life he was ashamed of. It represented bad decisions and loneliness. He appreciated his family like never before. He looked forward to the time he could spend with them. He went to Jason's football games, helped with driving Janet and Cindy to activities and helped them with their homework. They had family dinner night as often as possible and Greg always said the blessing. He always remembered to thank God for his family.

For Faith forgiveness was like taking a step from the past into the present. The future was indistinct and a little scary, but she wouldn't worry about that. With God's help she would face each day as it came and walk in His Grace.

One night Faith and Greg found themselves alone in the living room. Faith looked into Greg's eyes and saw the man she had fallen in love with so many years ago. He was a wonderful man. He was a sinner, just like everyone else. What he had done was devastating. But she knew he was worth a second chance. Working through this was infinitely more desirable than life without him. She would walk into an uncertain future in truth and faith, trusting that at last her whole family was resting in the hands of God.

CHAPTER 20

New Beginnings

F aith woke to the ringing telephone. It was 2:00 in the morning, It was late even for a call from France.

"Mom! It's time!" Jason sounded breathless. He and Marcia had been taking turns staying at each other's house. They would joke about who's house they would be at when Marcia went into labor.

"It's time? The baby's coming? How's Marcia?"

"She's doing better than I am. Her water broke, she just started having contractions. We're heading to the hospital."

I'll be right there."

"Can you let dad know?"

"Sure, honey. Calm down, you're ready for this. Everything will be fine."

"I know, I'll see you at the hospital."

Faith flew into action. First called Helen and asked her to come over and bring Janet and Cindy to the hospital after they woke up. Then she went downstairs and woke Greg. They met in the foyer ten minutes later and headed out the door.

Marcia's parents were at the hospital when they arrived.

They each went in to talk to the young couple. They talked about being grandparents. It was the first time for all of them. The Jones and the Griffins were becoming comfortable around each other.

"I remember what it was like when Marcia was born," said Meg.

"Cindy was my last baby. It doesn't seem like it was that long ago. It's hard to believe our kids are going to be parent's, isn't it? This waiting is just as hard a delivering," said Faith.

"I doubt if Marcia and Jason would agree. It's funny how we forget the pain, isn't it? I remember that it hurt but I can't remember how much," said Meg.

"I think God, in His infinite wisdom, made sure that women wouldn't have to live with the memory. I remember every second of waiting. It's hard on husbands, too. What a helpless feeling to watch someone you love hurting and not be able to do anything to help," said Greg.

"Well, I have to do something. I'm going for a cup of coffee," said Faith. "Anyone else want one?"

"Sure," they all said in unison.

"I'll go with you," said Greg. "To help carry."

Their footsteps echoed as they walked down the hallway. Greg's presence was tangible. Faith ached for the past when she could turn to him for support.

"I keep remembering when we were here, having our kids. I wish we could go back there and try again. There are so many things I would do different," said Greg.

"I was thinking of back then, too. I had such high hopes."

Greg took her hand and they stopped walking. Outside they could see the rooftops of the city. He turned to her and she to him. He took her other hand and looked deeply into her eyes.

"Faith, I am so, so sorry." His eyes filled with water and one tear ran down his face. "I know it doesn't help but I just have to say it. What an idiot I am, I was. I miss you."

"I miss you, too, Greg. I miss the man I thought you were."

"Let me try to make it up to you. Let me try to be the man you thought I was. At least let me hold you. Let's get through this together. We're a family, Faith. We may be a fragmented one, at the moment, but we are a family." Greg put his arms around her and just like at Christmas, Faith allowed his strength to envelop her, for a few moments. Then he held her at arm's length and they looked in each other's eyes again, at the love and longing. Time stood still. And he bent down, and he kissed her. It was a familiar kiss and yet it was new. It had been well over a year since the last time their lips met. She desperately wanted to believe in him, but how could she?

They got coffee and walked back to the waiting room.

"The nurse came out to tell us that they've moved Marcia to delivery," said Meg.

"I hope the rest goes fast, for her sake," said Faith.

Two hours later the nurse came back to let them know that they were the grandparents of a beautiful baby girl. They were able to say hi and see the baby. Faith was struck by the evidence of love that was all around her.

She saw it in the Griffins who were leaning over one side of the bed, looking with love at Marcia and the baby.

She saw it in her son's eyes when he looked at Marcia and their baby girl.

And she saw the love in Greg's eyes when he looked at her.

Her heart responded to that look and the last of the walls came down. She knew in that moment that she could save her marriage and keep her family together. If other people did it, she could, too. She would find a way.